Heroes vs. Villains

By Billy Wrecks

Illustrated by Erik Doescher, Mike DeCarlo, and David Tanguay

Random House 🏠 New York

Copyright © 2013 DC Comics.
DC SUPER FRIENDS and all related characters
and elements are trademarks of and © DC Comics.
WB SHIELD: TM & © Warner Bros. Entertainment Inc.
(s13)

RHUS26394

Published in the United States by Random House Children's Books, a division of Random House, Inc.,
1745 Broadway, New York, NY 10019, and in Canada by Random House of Canada Limited, Toronto.
ISBN: 978-0-307-97616-1   randomhouse.com/kids   dckids.kidswb.com   MANUFACTURED IN CHINA
10 9 8 7 6 5 4 3 2

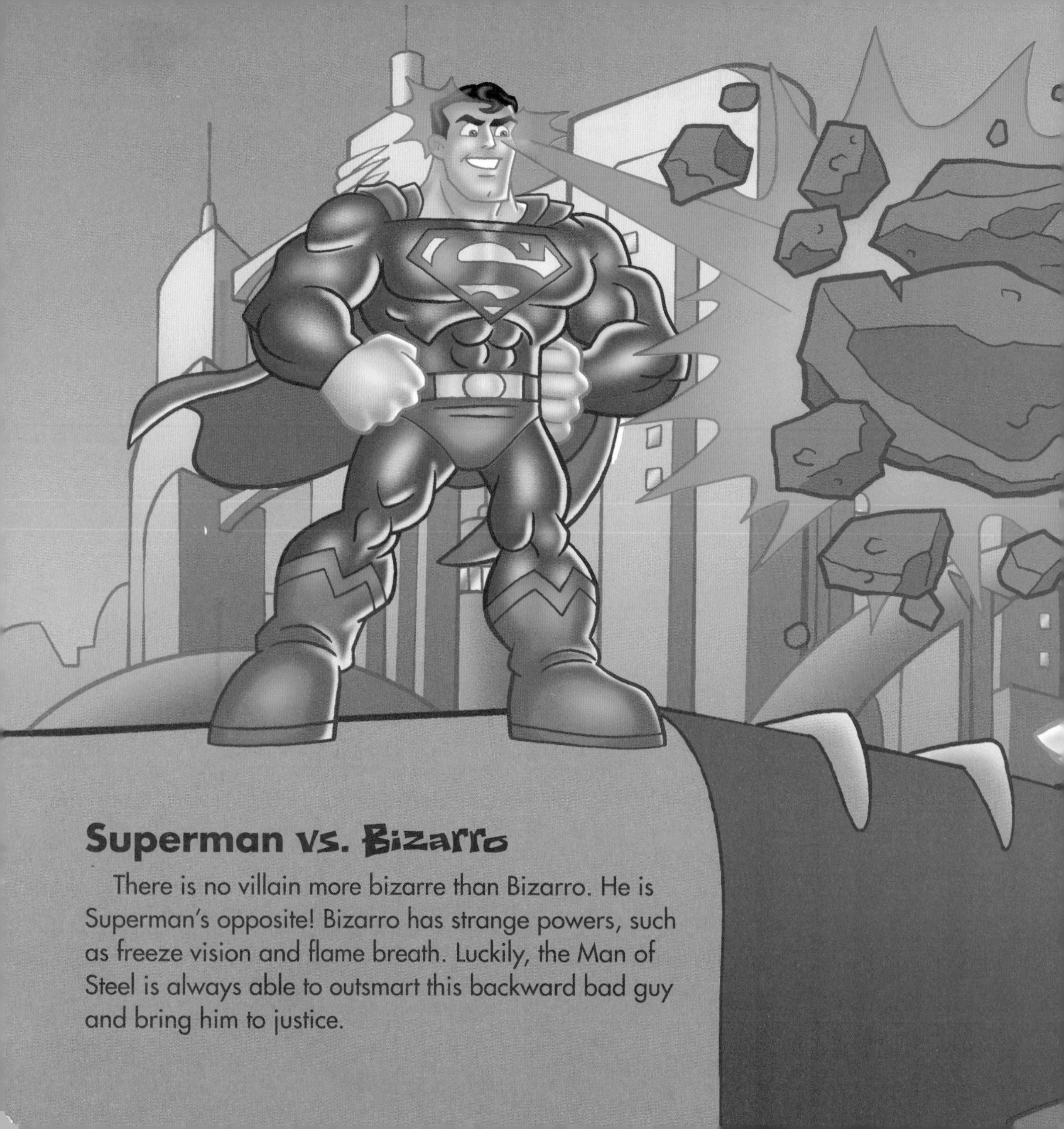

Superman vs. Bizarro

There is no villain more bizarre than Bizarro. He is Superman's opposite! Bizarro has strange powers, such as freeze vision and flame breath. Luckily, the Man of Steel is always able to outsmart this backward bad guy and bring him to justice.

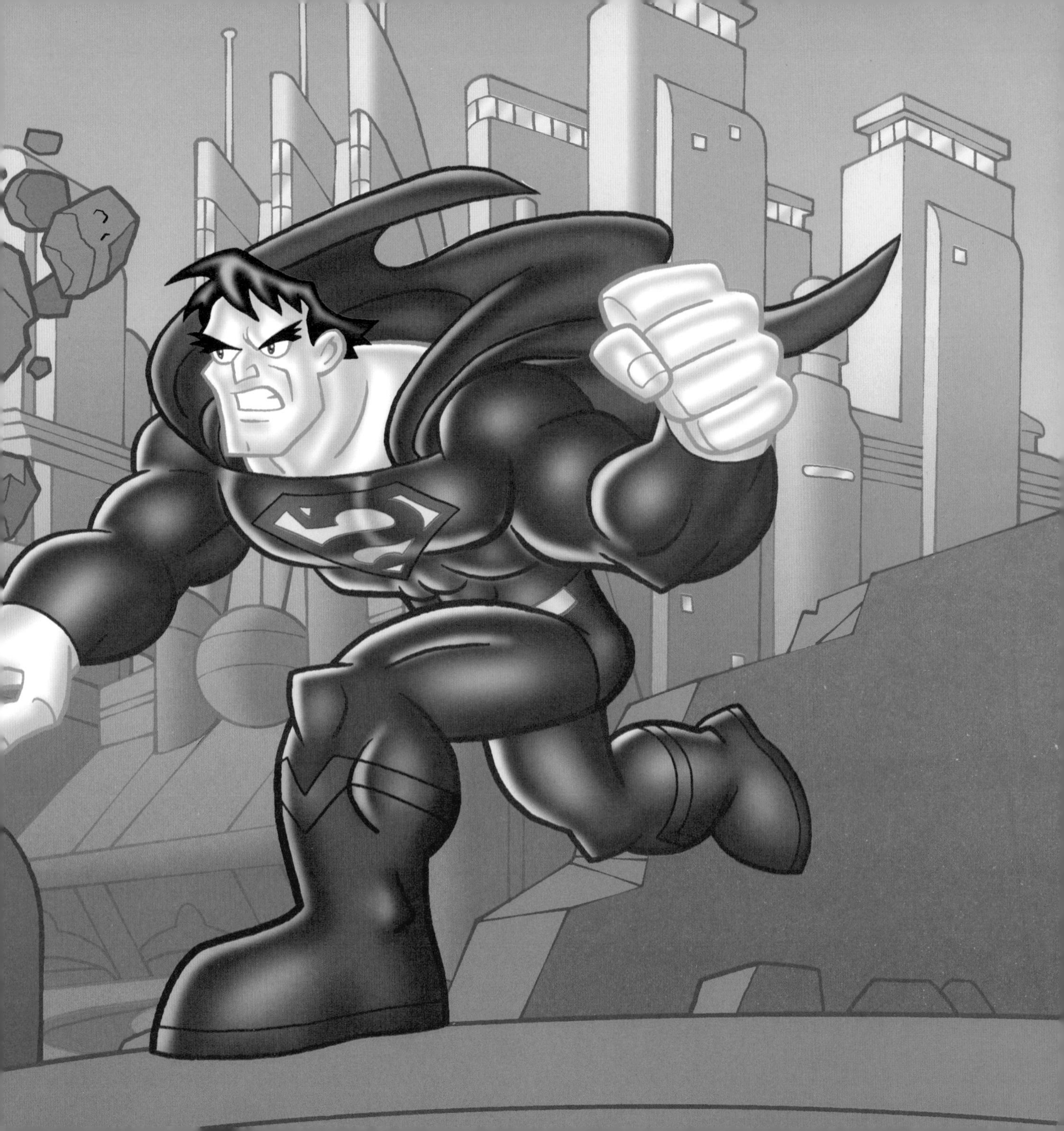

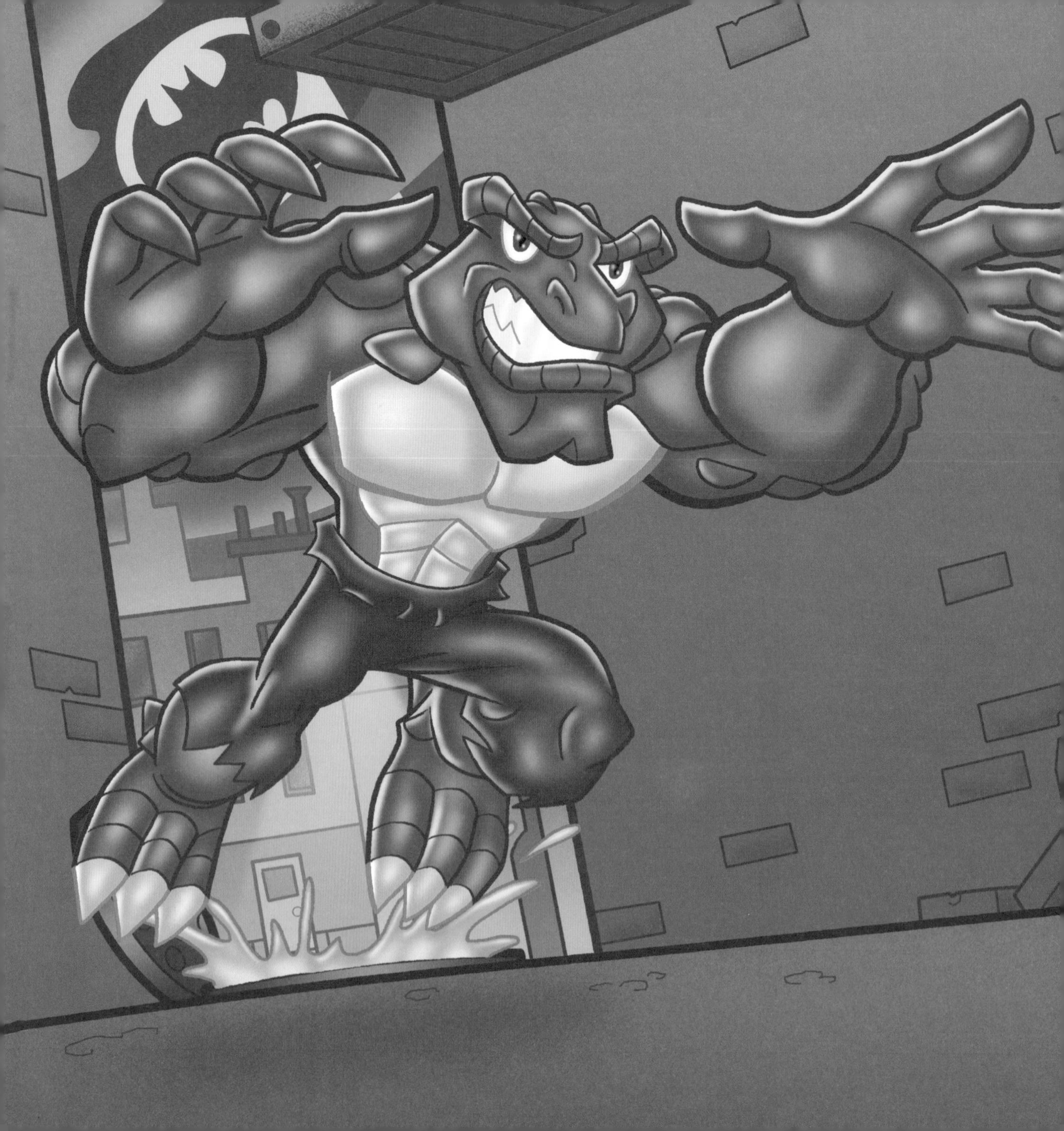

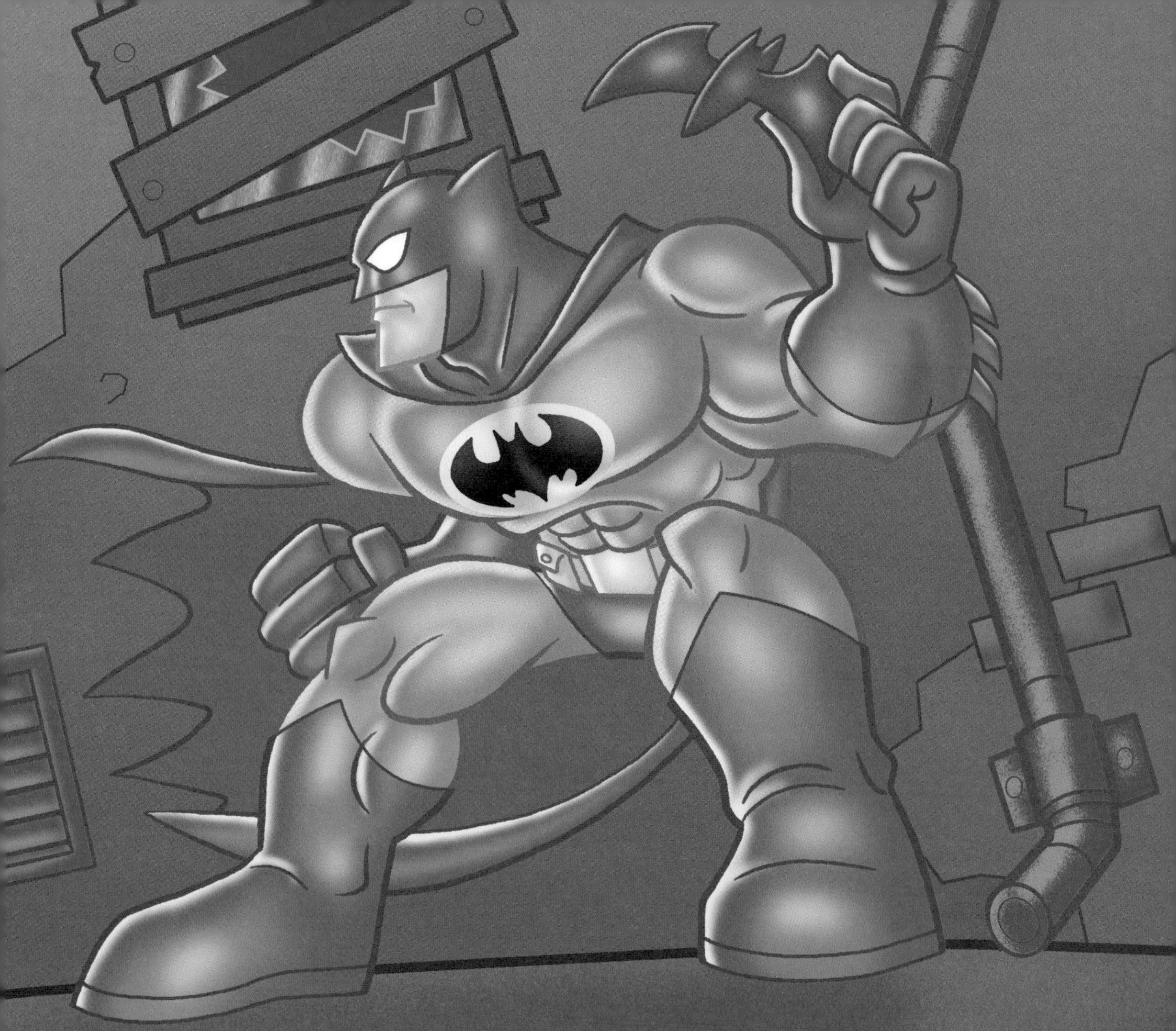

Batman vs. Croc

Cold-blooded Croc uses his brute strength and deadly jaws to commit his crimes. But even Croc's tough, lizardlike skin is no match for Batman's quick thinking and awesome arsenal of high-tech gadgets.

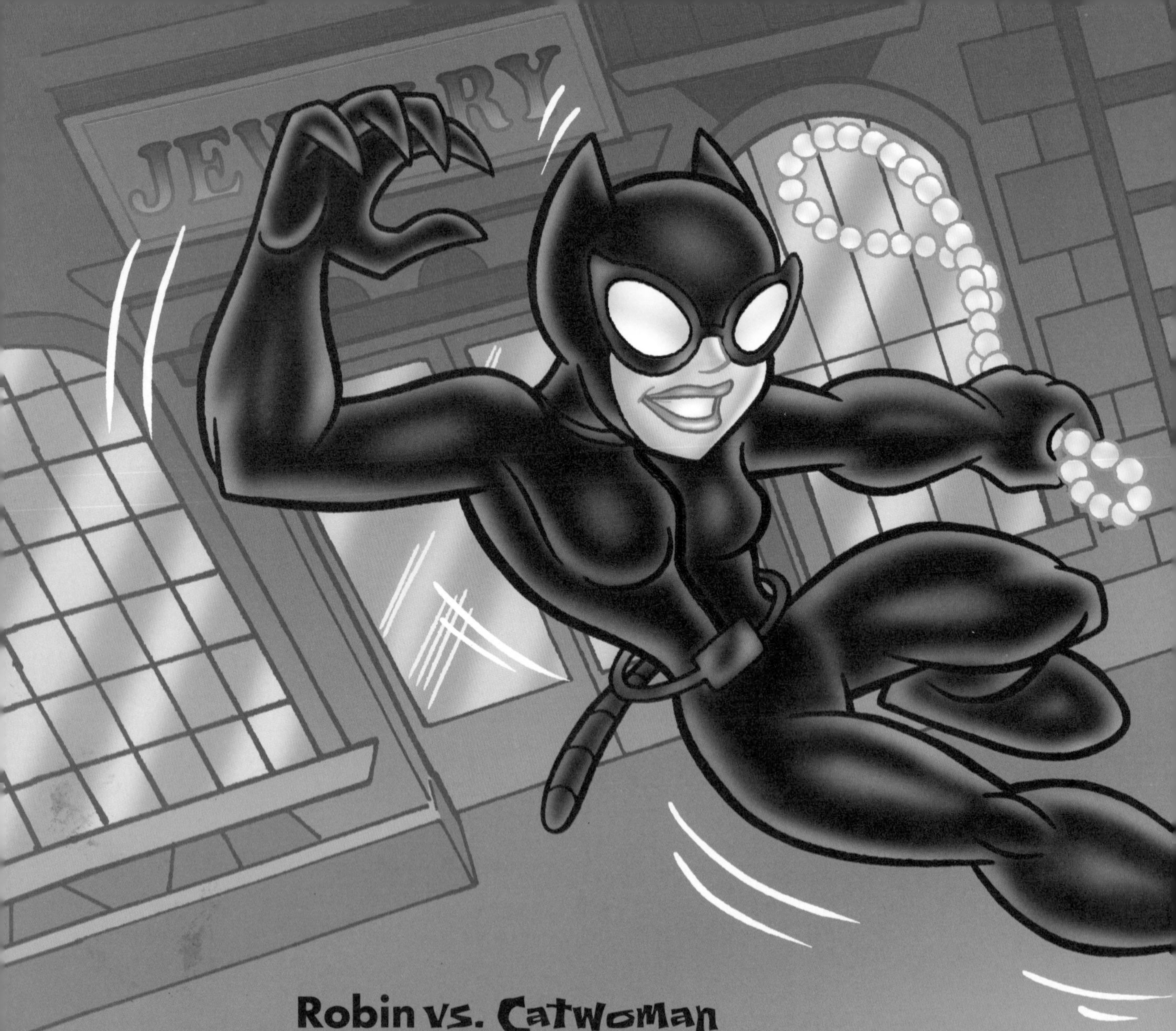
JEWELRY

Robin vs. Catwoman

Catwoman is a burglar who uses her catlike reflexes to slip in and out of tight places when she heists Gotham City's most precious jewels. Robin relies on his own amazing acrobatic skills to avoid Catwoman's razor-sharp claws—and put this criminal kitten back in her cage.

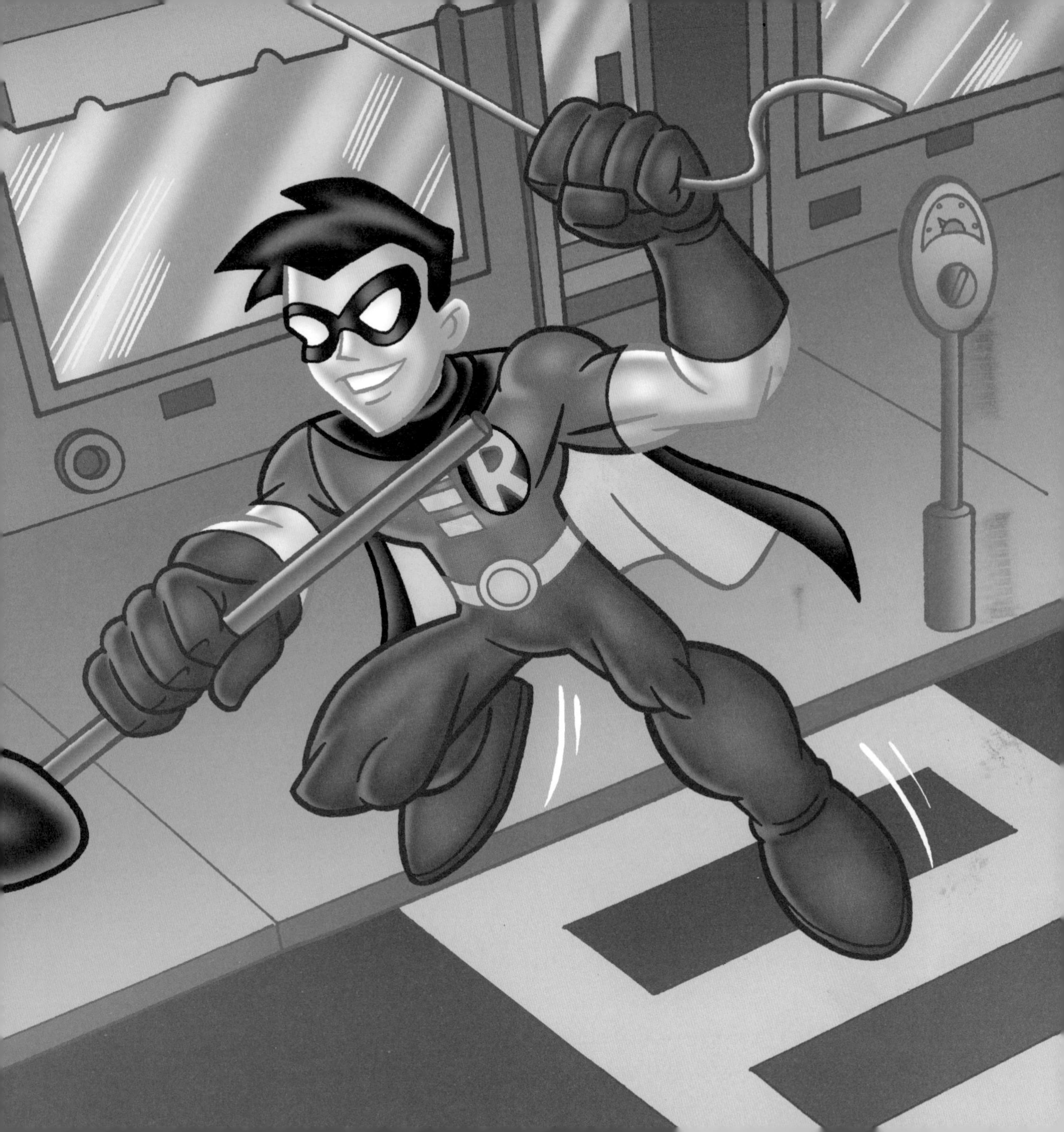

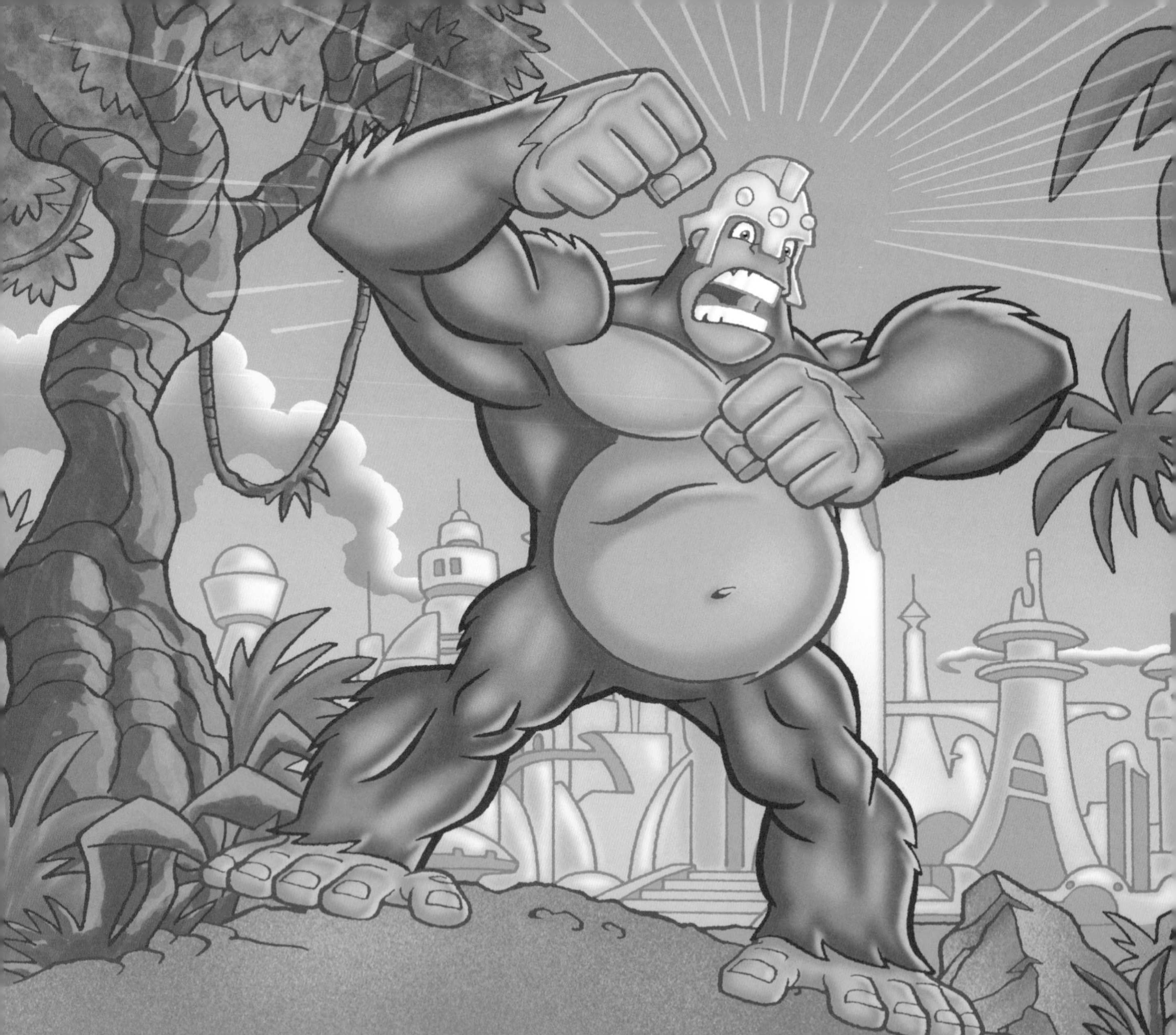

The Flash vs. Gorilla Grodd

Gorilla Grodd uses his super-strength, his super-intelligence, and his mind-control helmet to try to take over the world—and make himself top banana! Super-fast Flash never monkeys around when he faces this awesome ape.

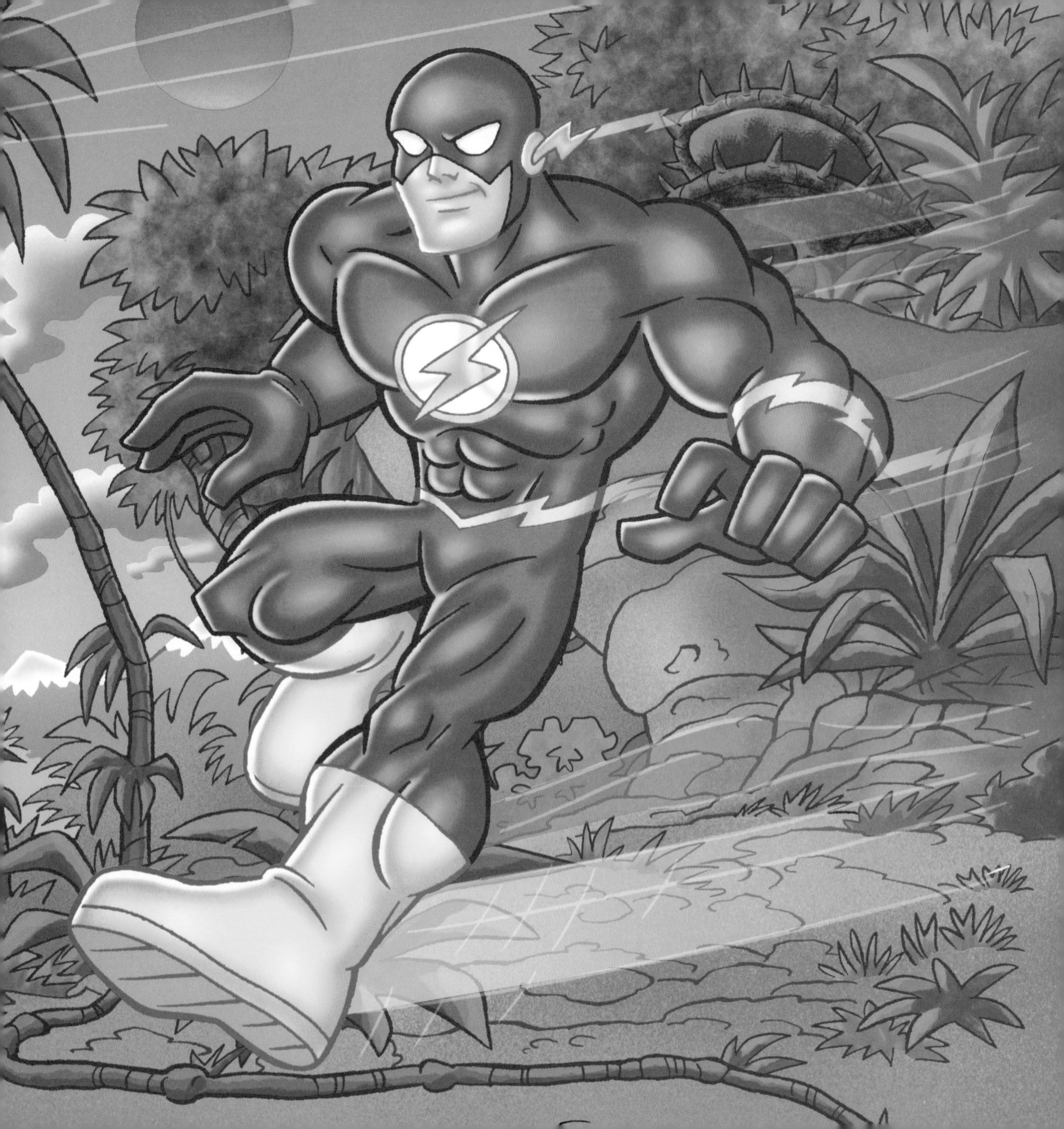

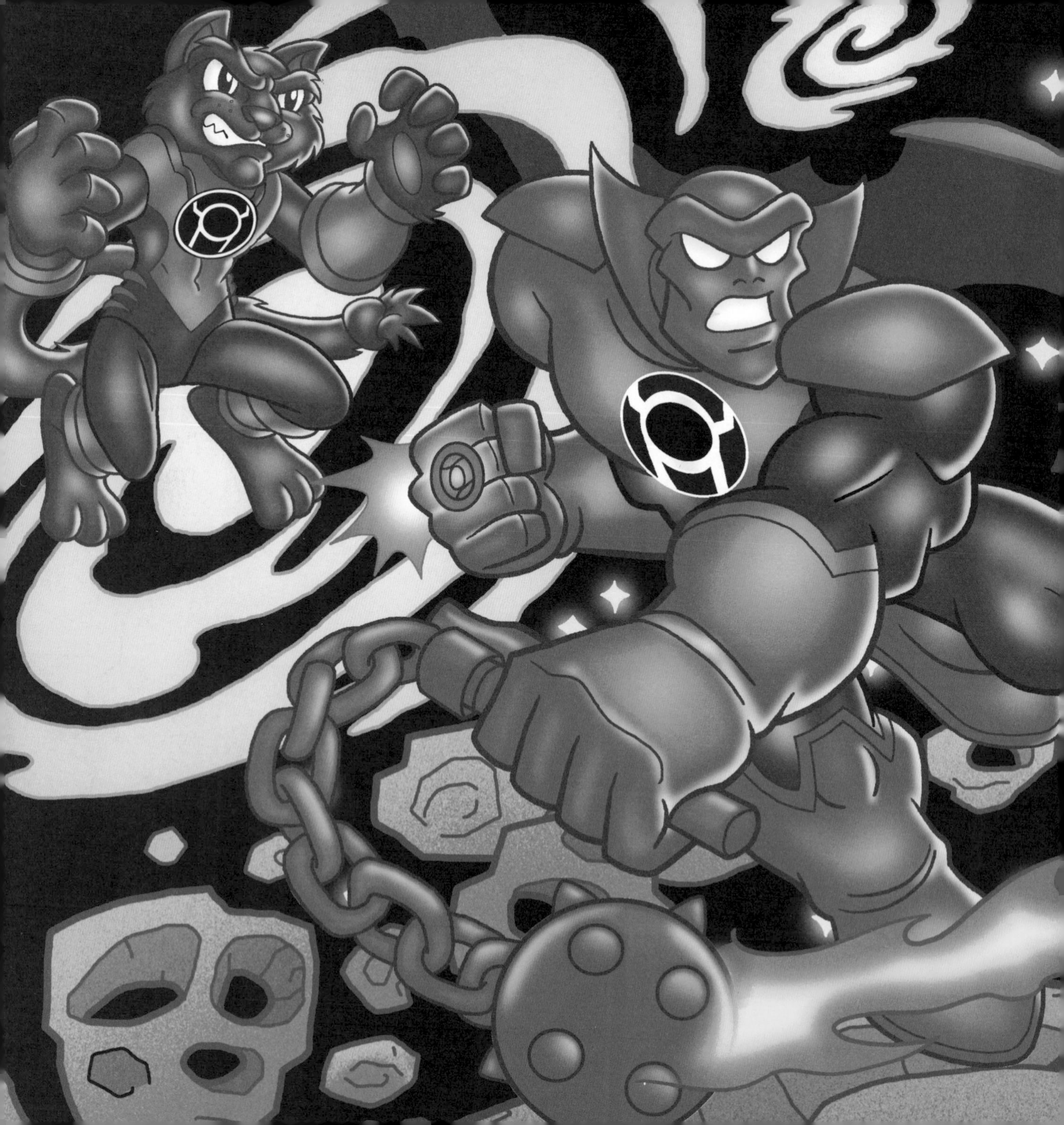

Green Lantern vs. Atrocitus

The alien Atrocitus wears a power ring that is fueled by his limitless anger. With his ring, Atrocitus can create anything he can imagine out of fiery red energy! Atrocitus is often aided by Dex-Starr, a mischievous cat whose cuteness hides a *purr*-fectly wicked heart! Luckily, Green Lantern is brave enough to stand up to these vicious villains and keep the universe safe from their hot-tempered appetite for destruction!

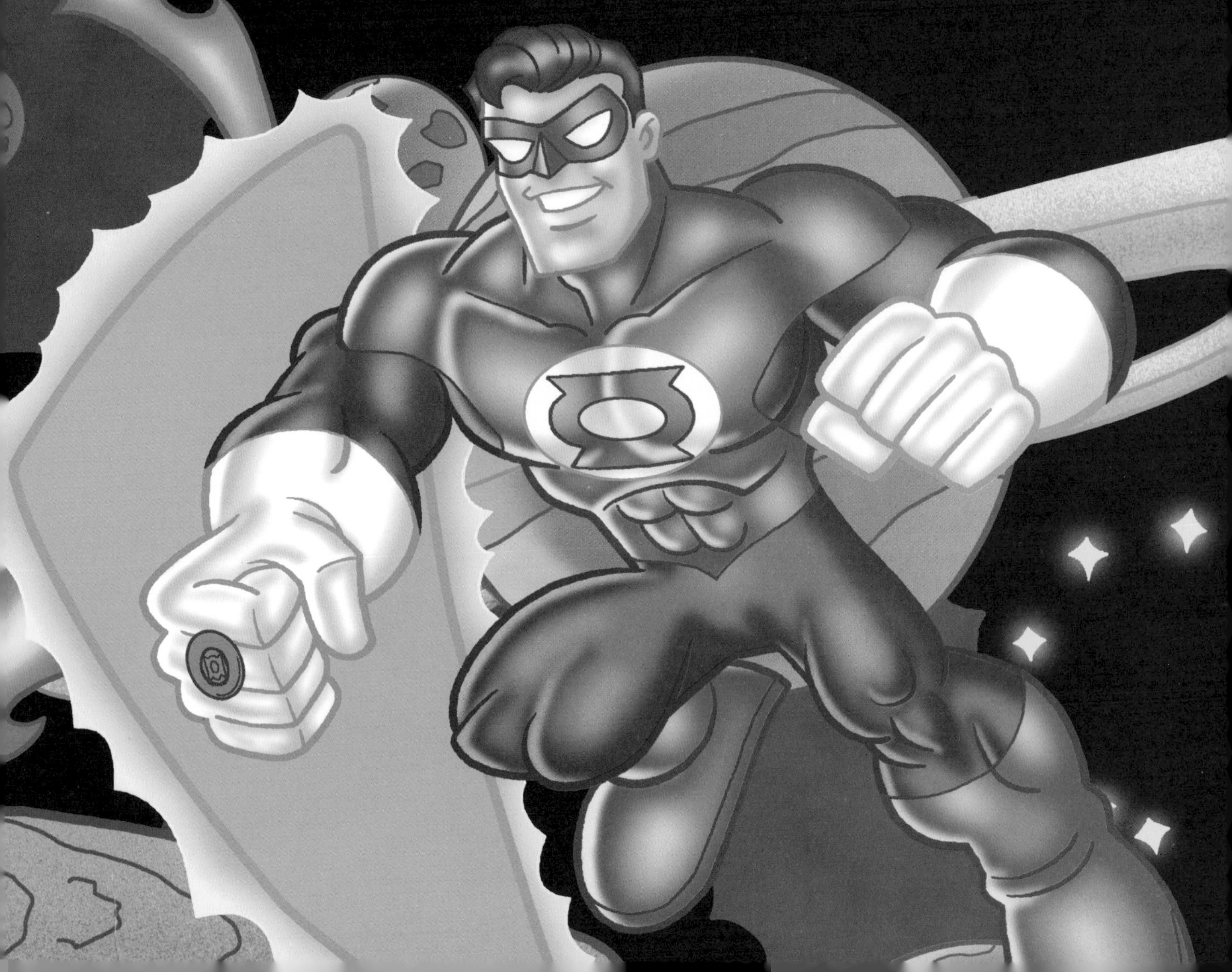

Aquaman vs. Black Manta

Black Manta wears a high-tech helmet and diving suit to swim in the deepest parts of the ocean. Only Aquaman, Ruler of Atlantis, keeps Black Manta from taking over the underwater world.

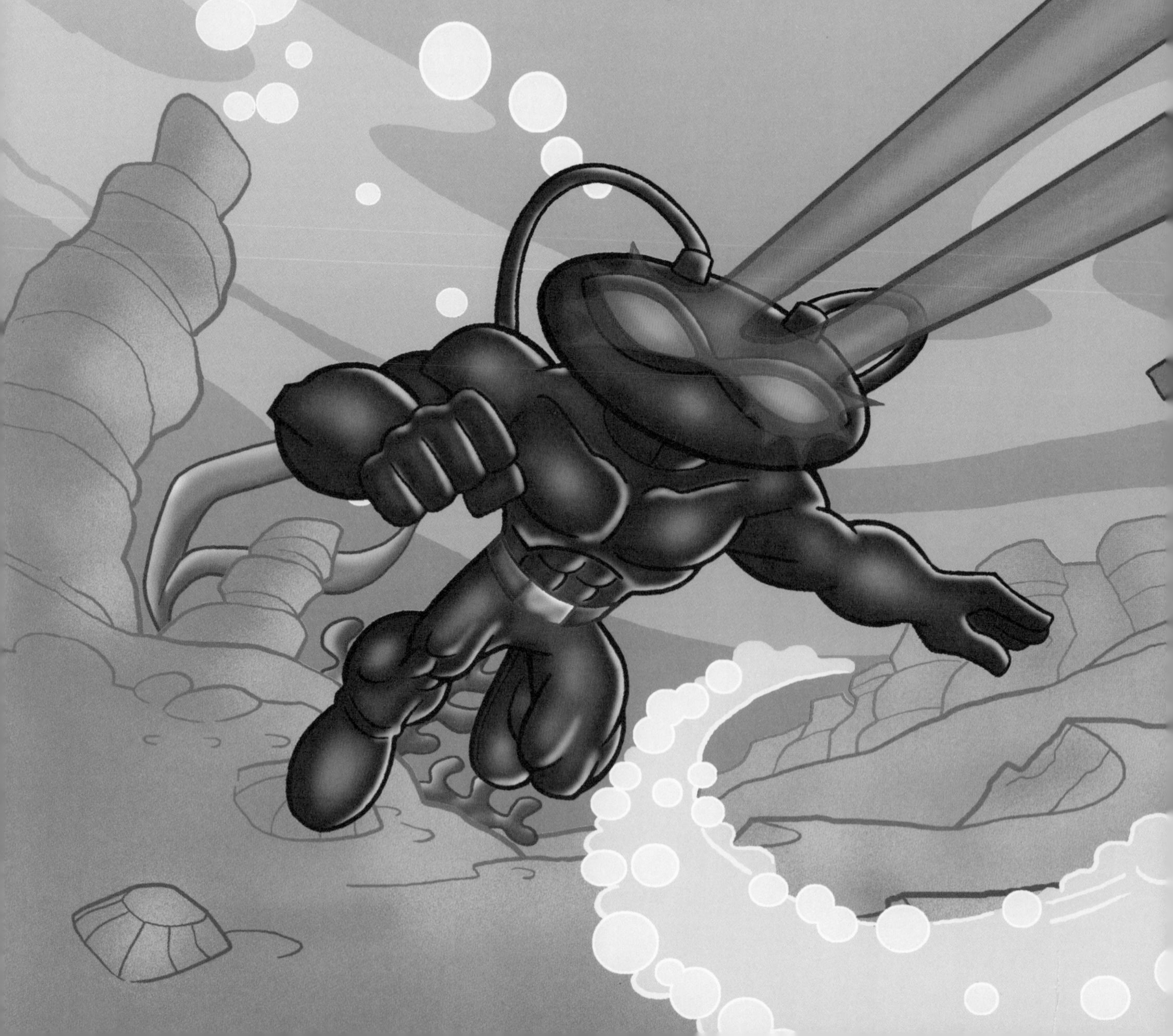

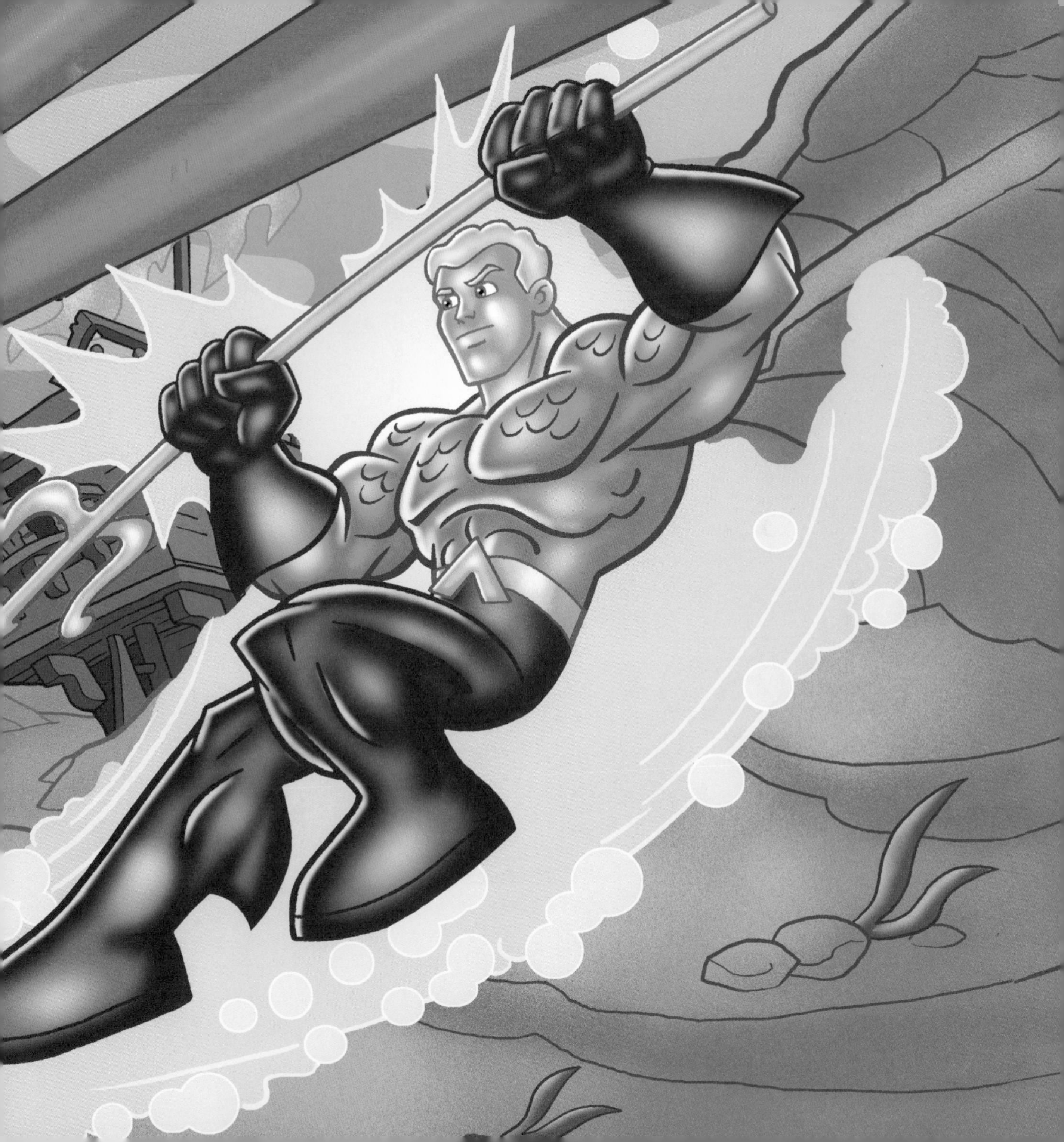

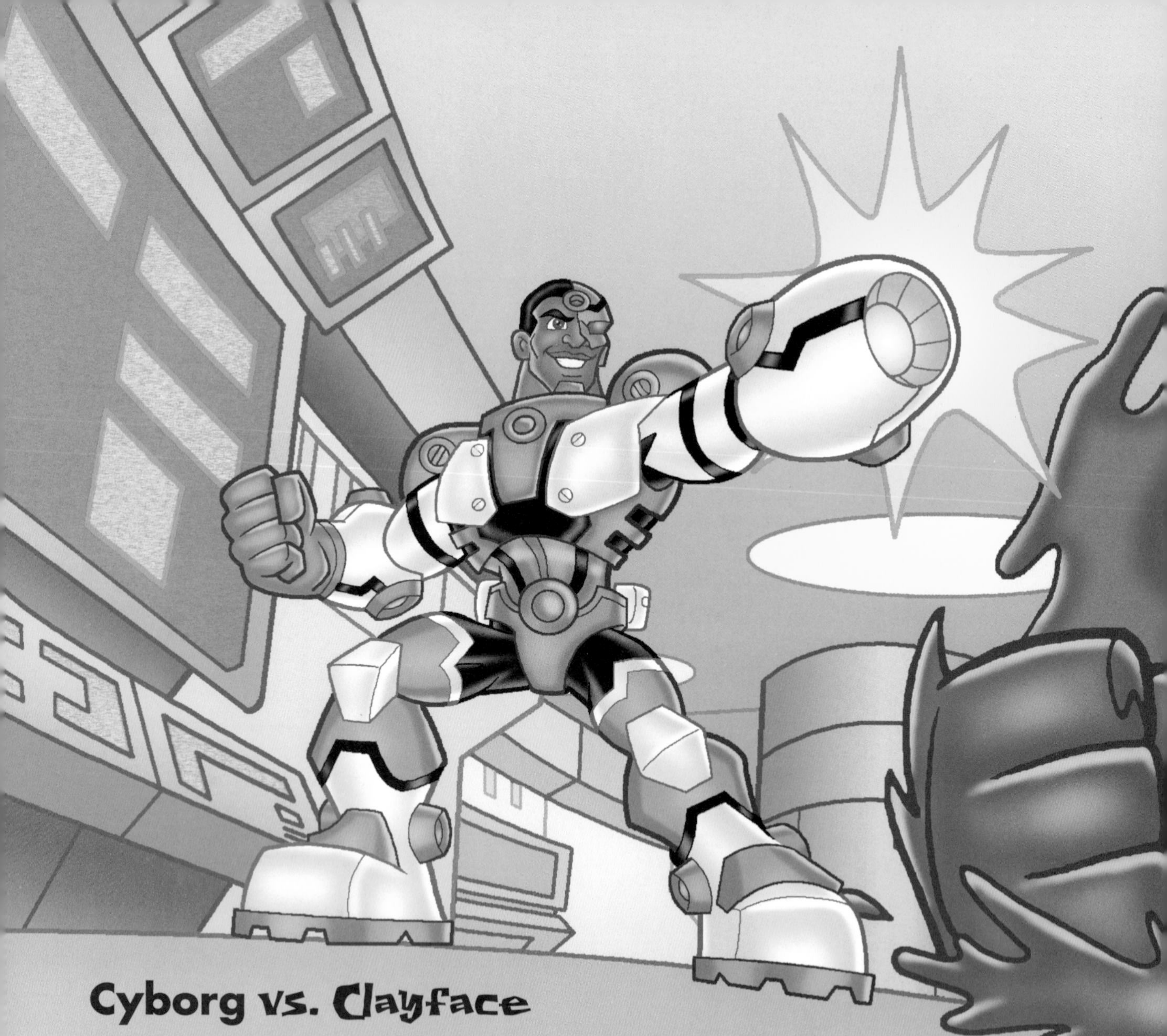

Cyborg vs. Clayface

Clayface is made out of living clay! He can squeeze through the tiniest openings to commit crimes and can use his *big* fists as destructive weapons! Luckily, Cyborg matches this malleable menace's every move with his amazing machine body.

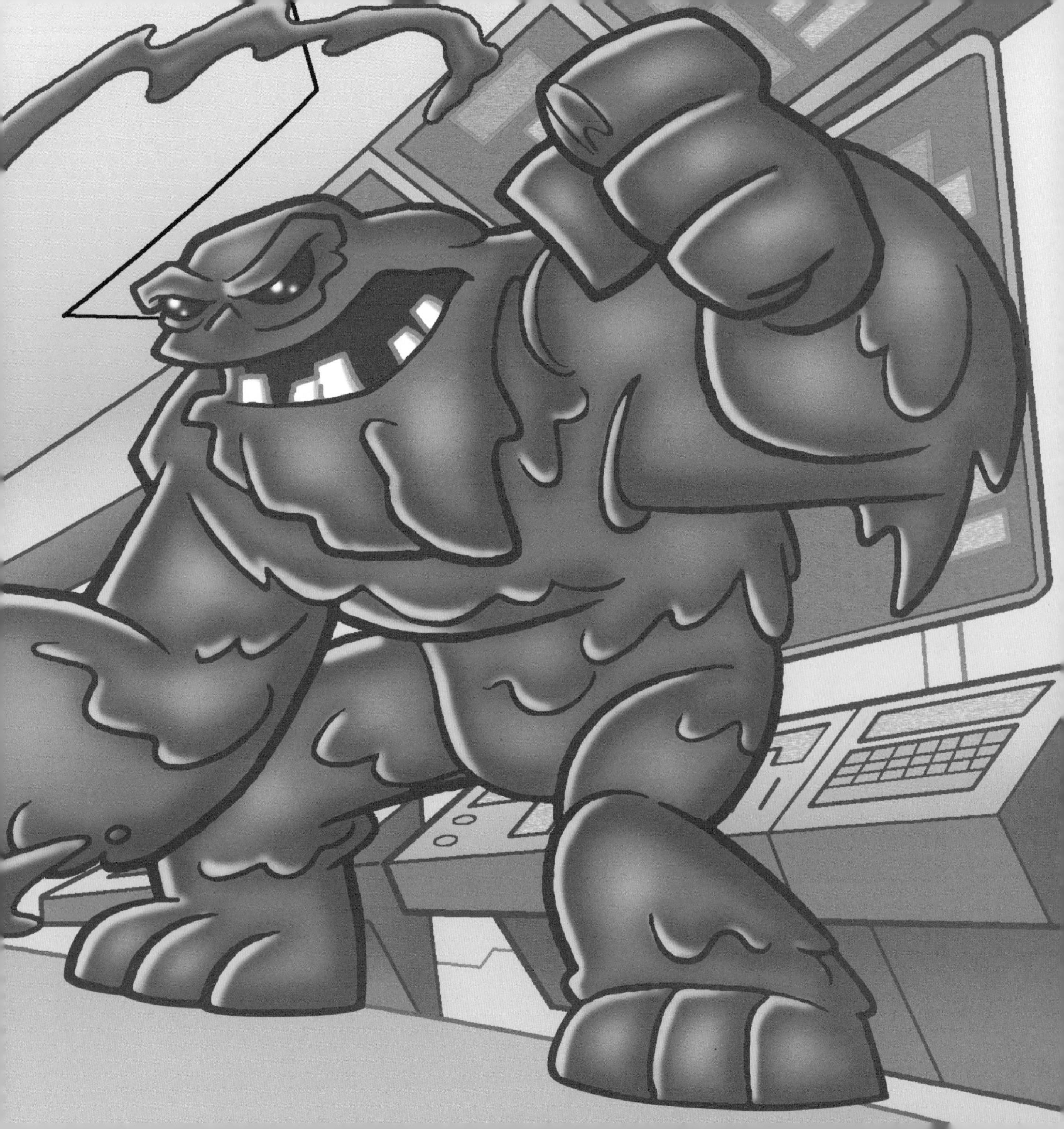

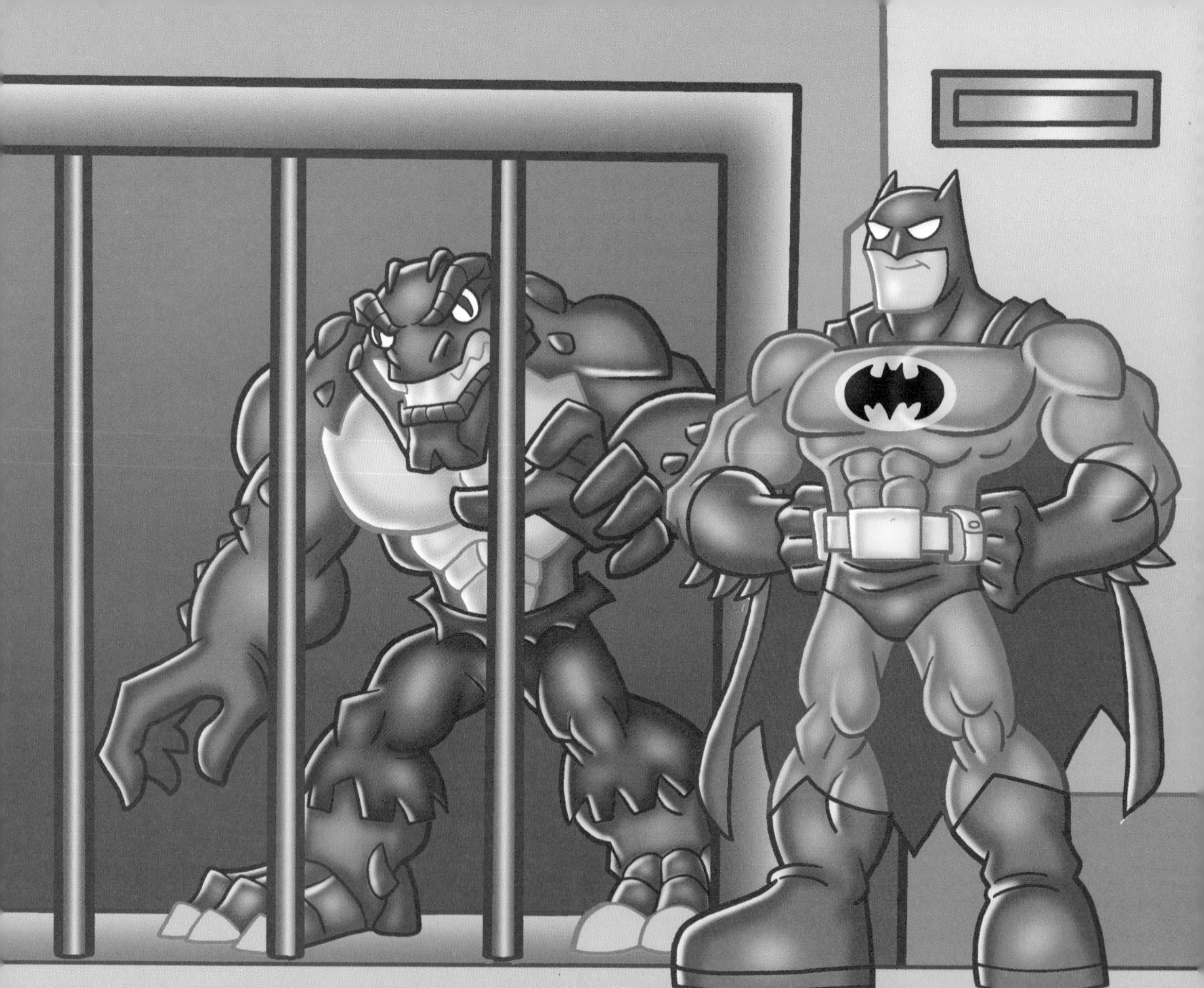

Heroes!

Thanks to Batman, Superman, and the rest of the Super Friends, the heroes always win, and the villains are stopped in their tracks!

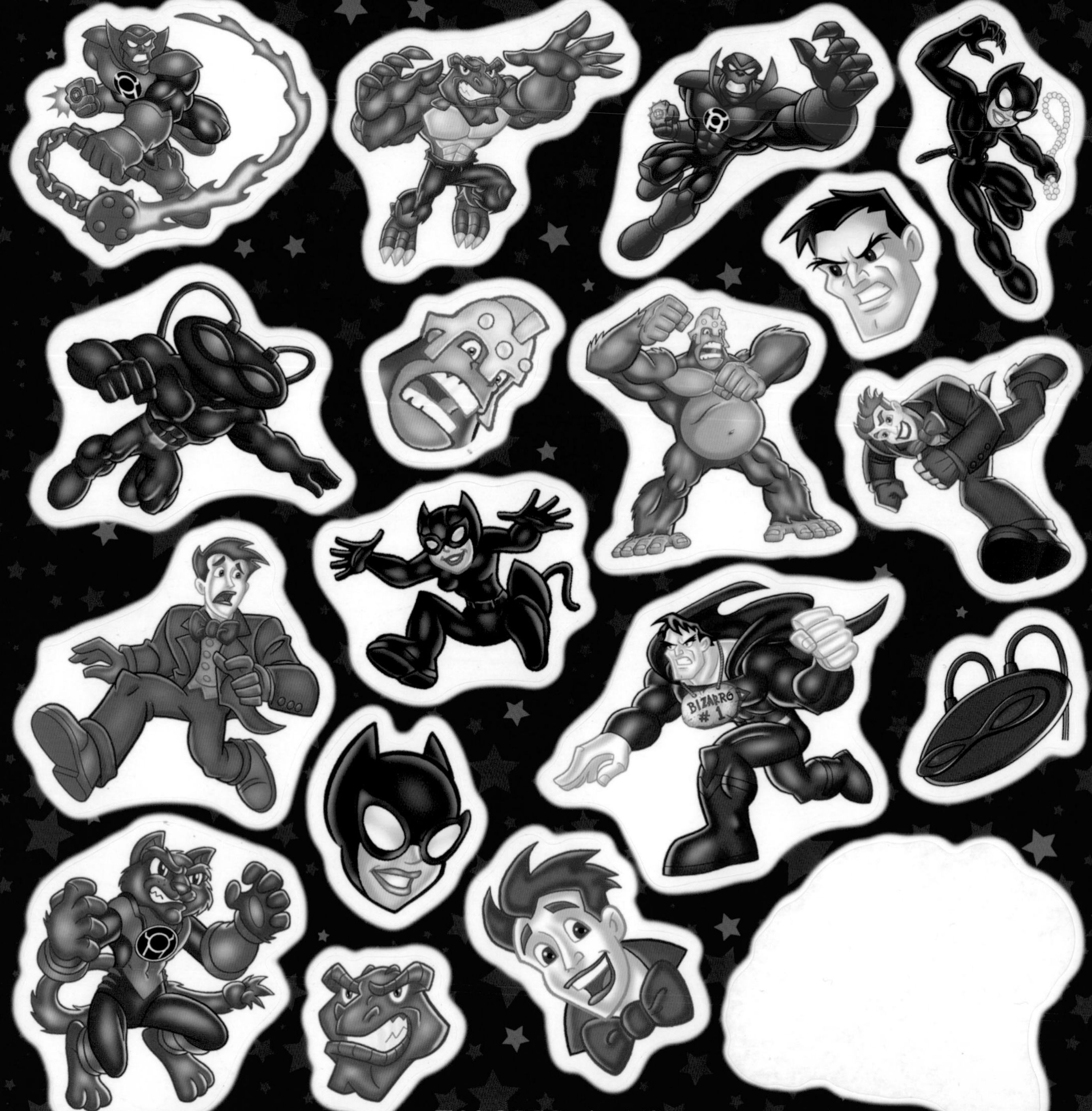
BIZARRO
1

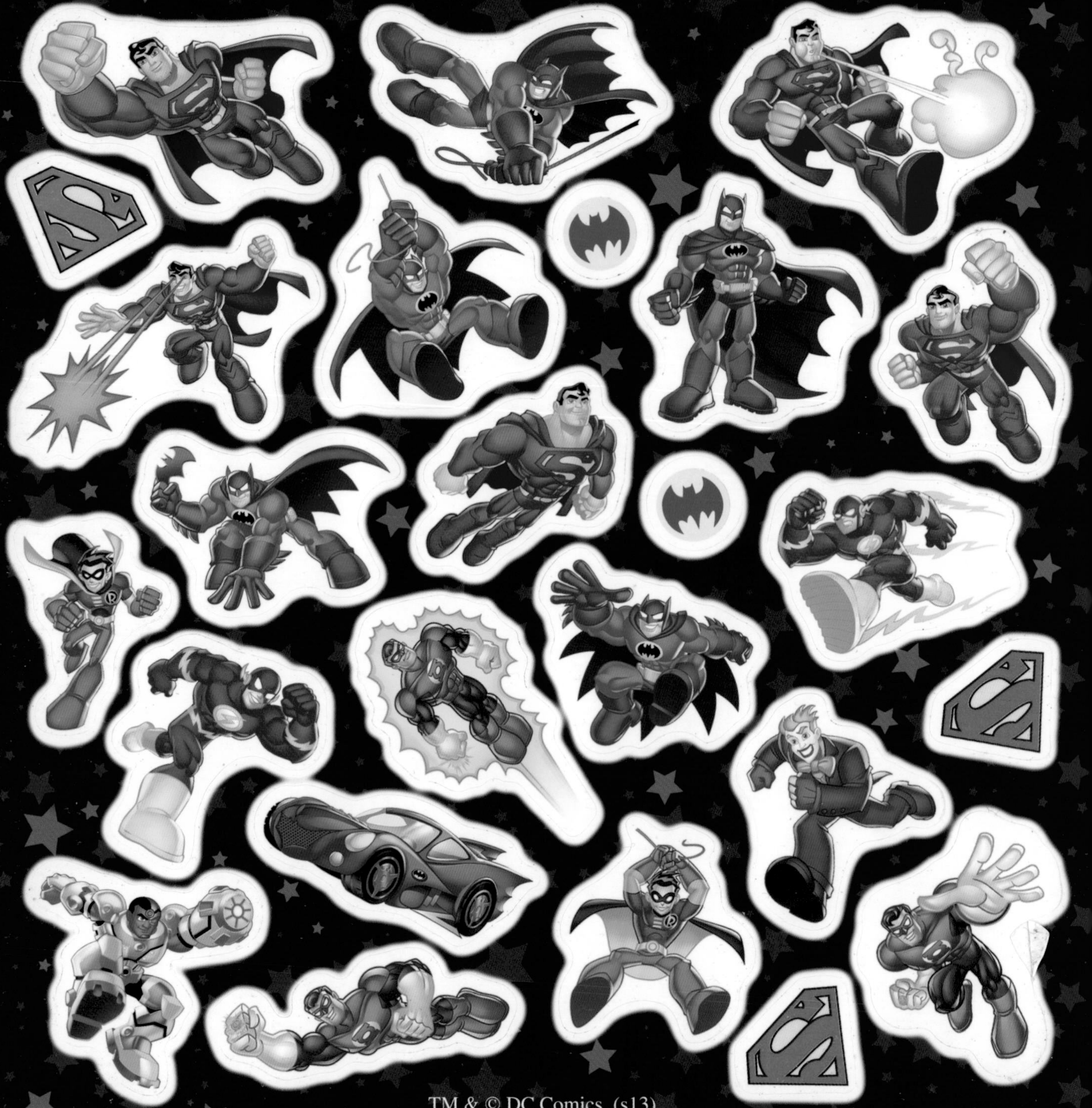

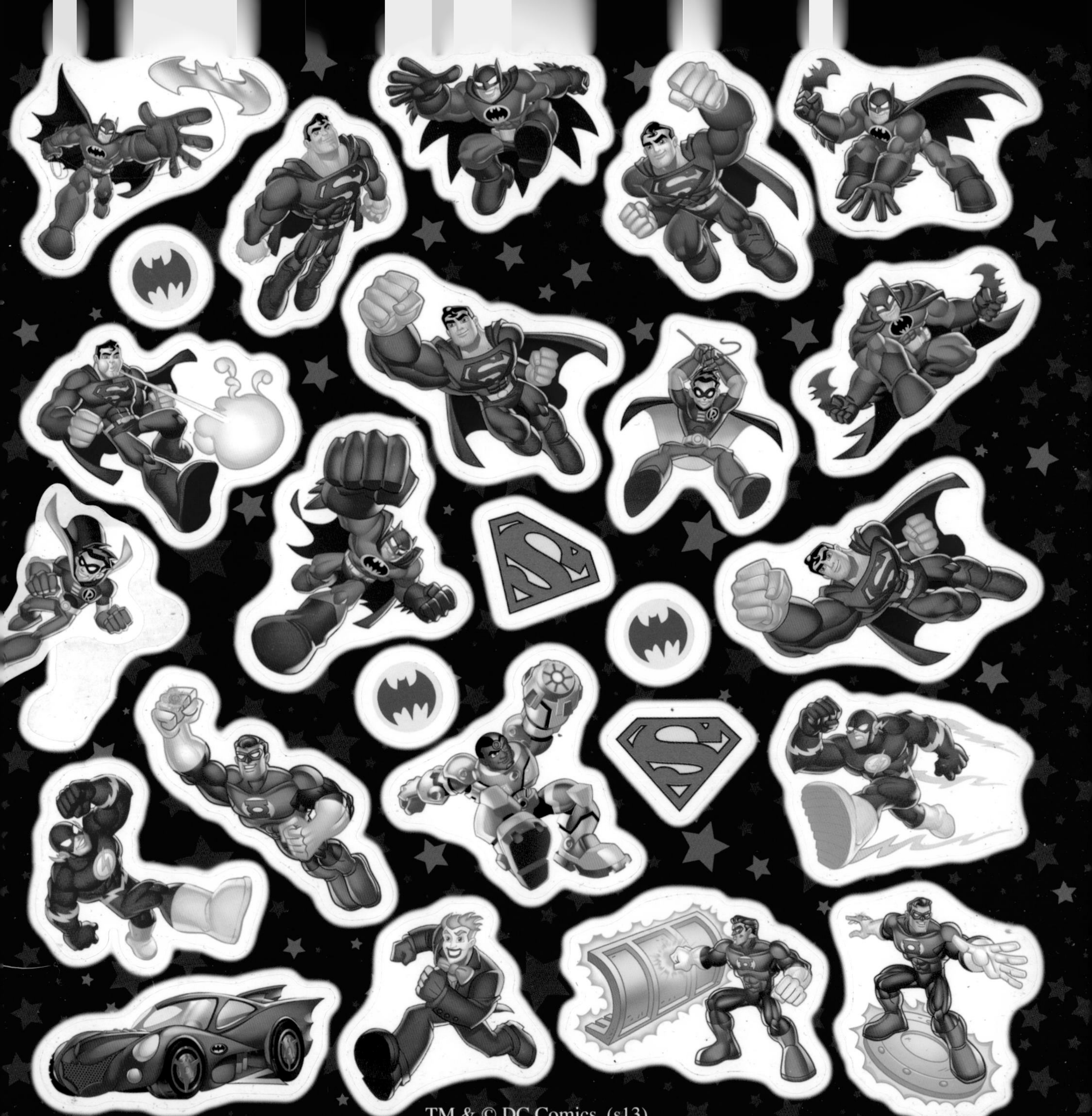

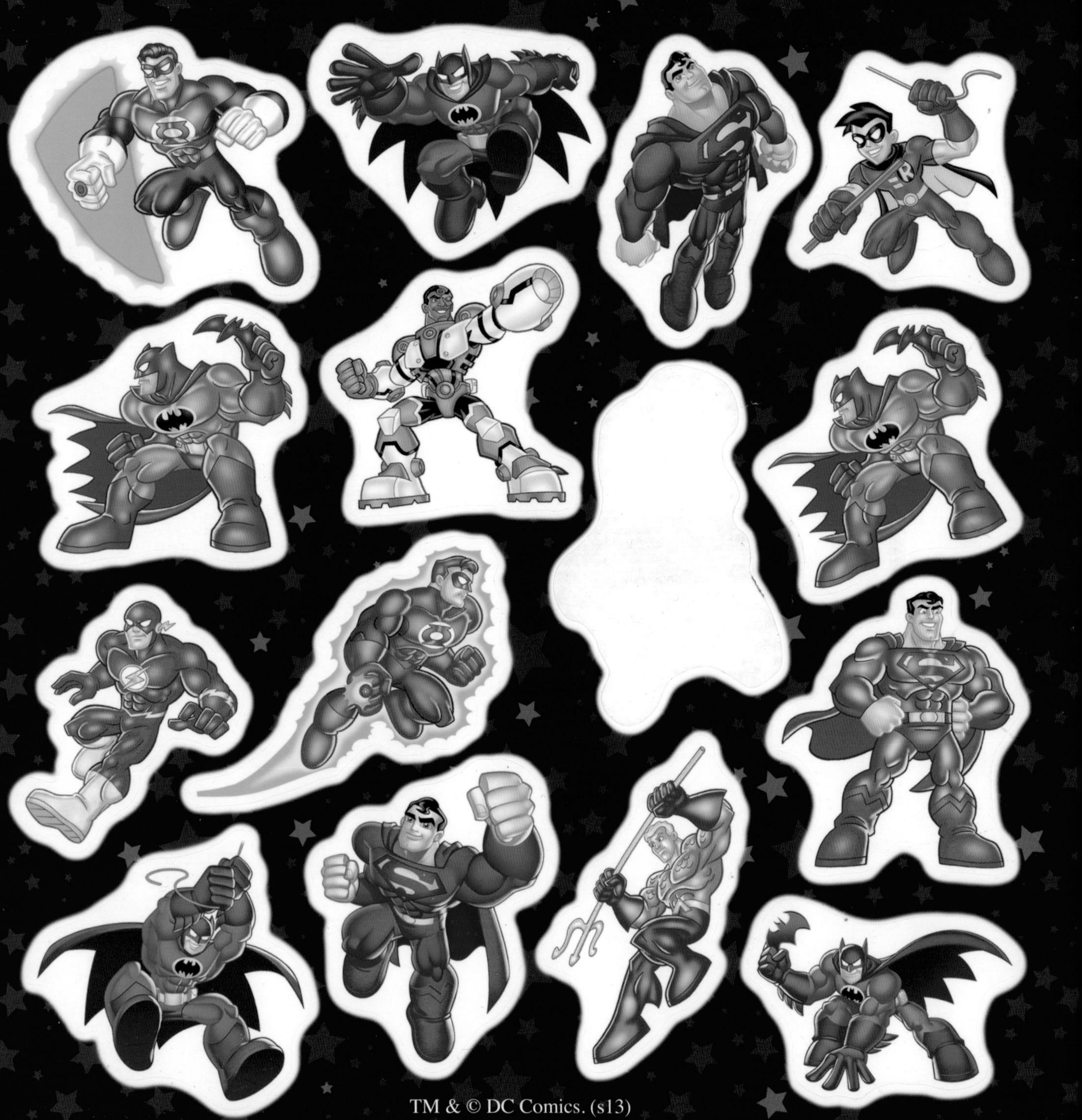

"You're canceled, Joker," said Batman.
"Stay tuned for a nice long stay in jail," added Superman.
"Good night, everybody," grumbled the criminal clown.

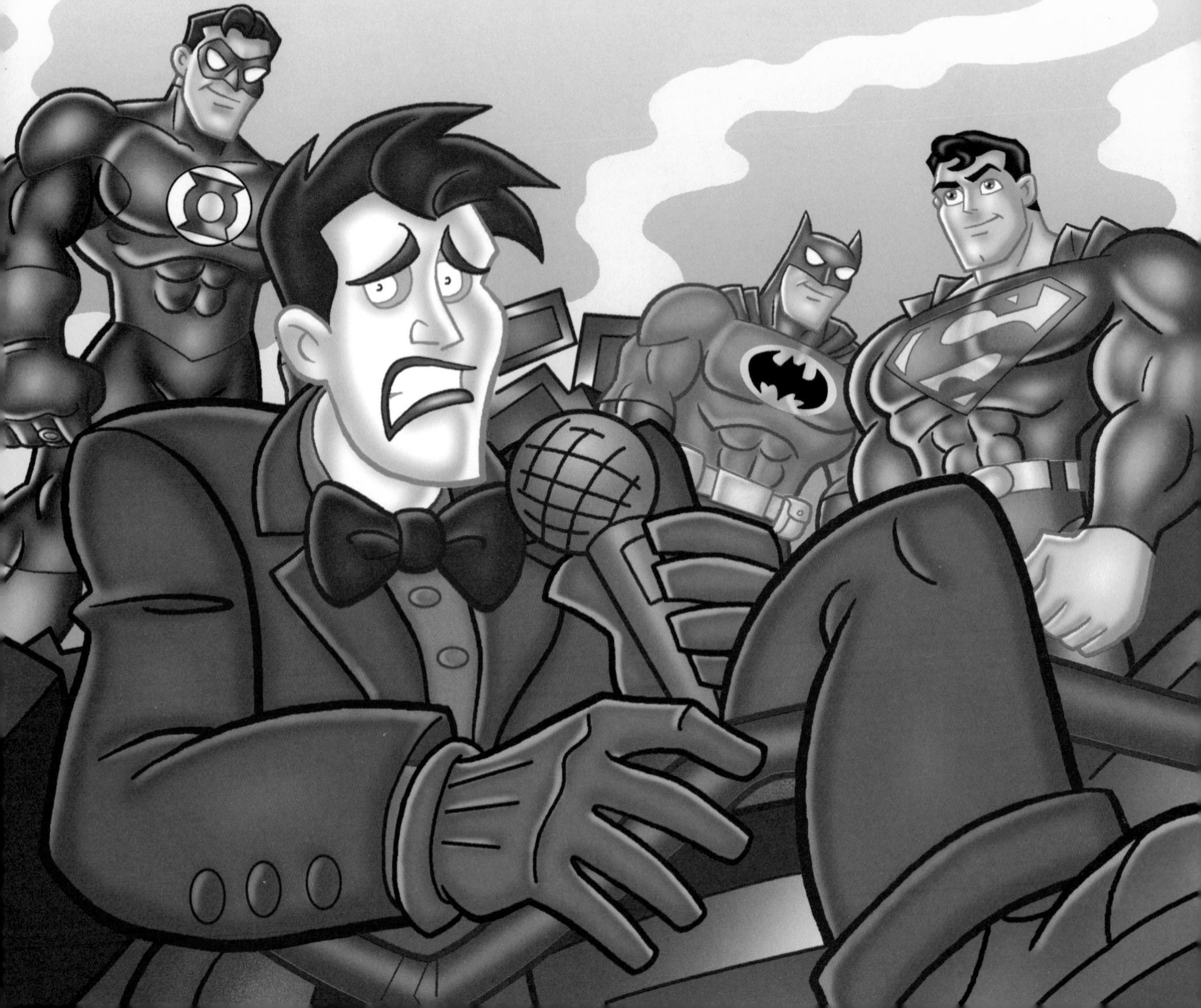

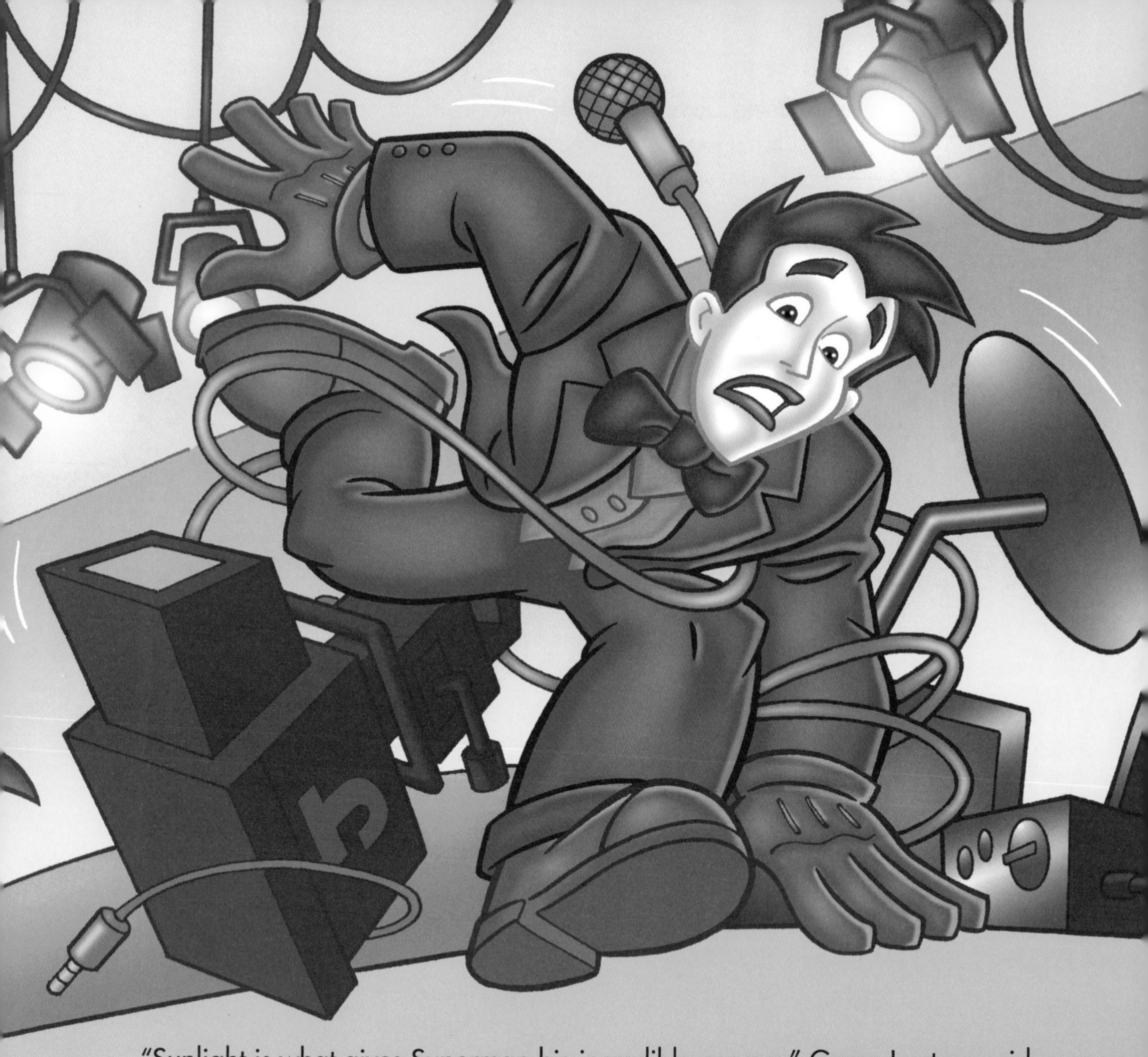

“Sunlight is what gives Superman his incredible powers,” Green Lantern said.

“With Batman’s quick thinking and Green Lantern’s power ring, I was able to get a big dose of sunlight and save everyone from your trap,” said Superman.

Just when the Joker thought he was getting away, Batman rolled a TV camera into his path—**WHUMP!**—and the Joker fell to the floor.

"How did you escape?" the Joker cried, shocked to see the heroes.

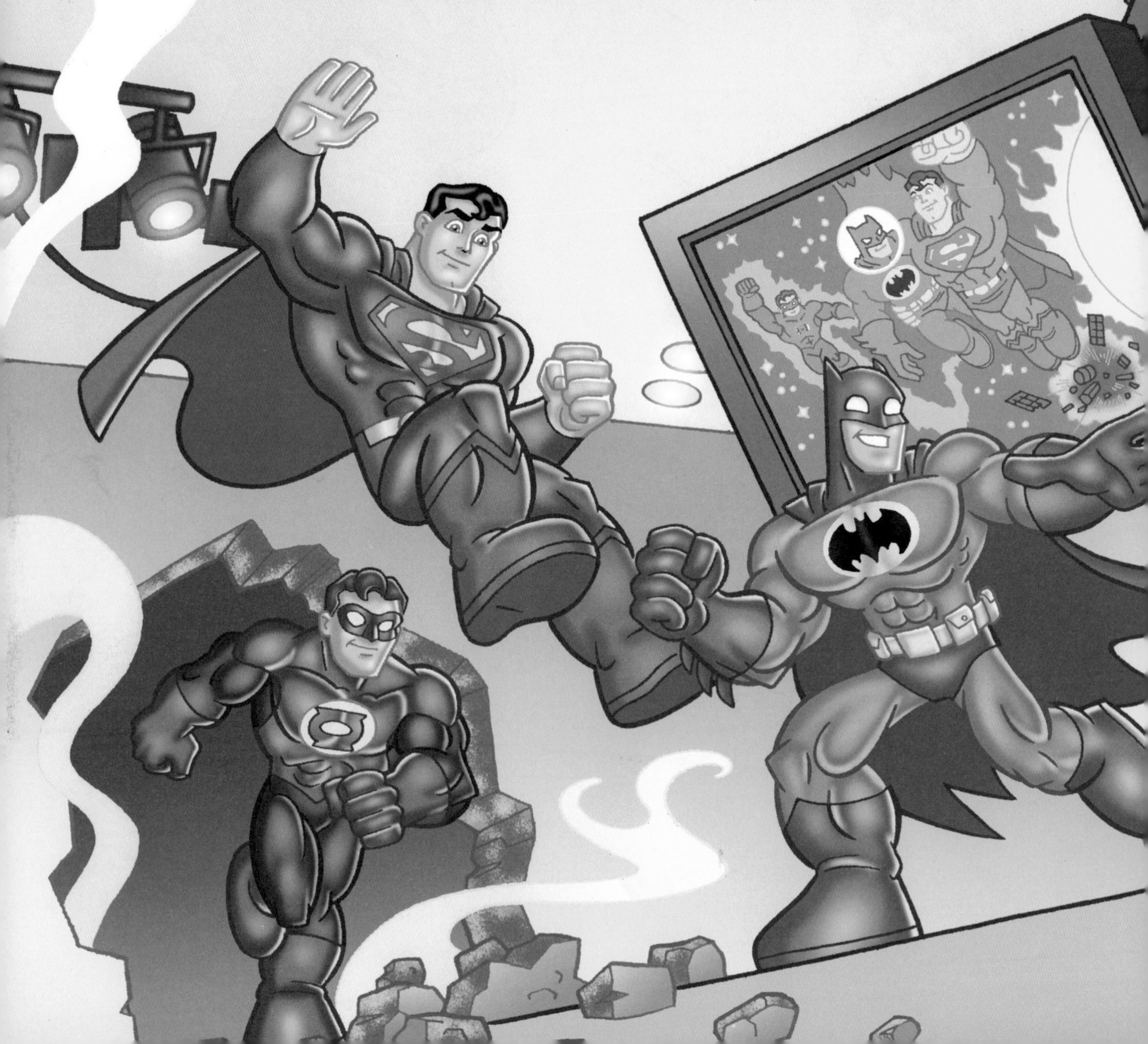

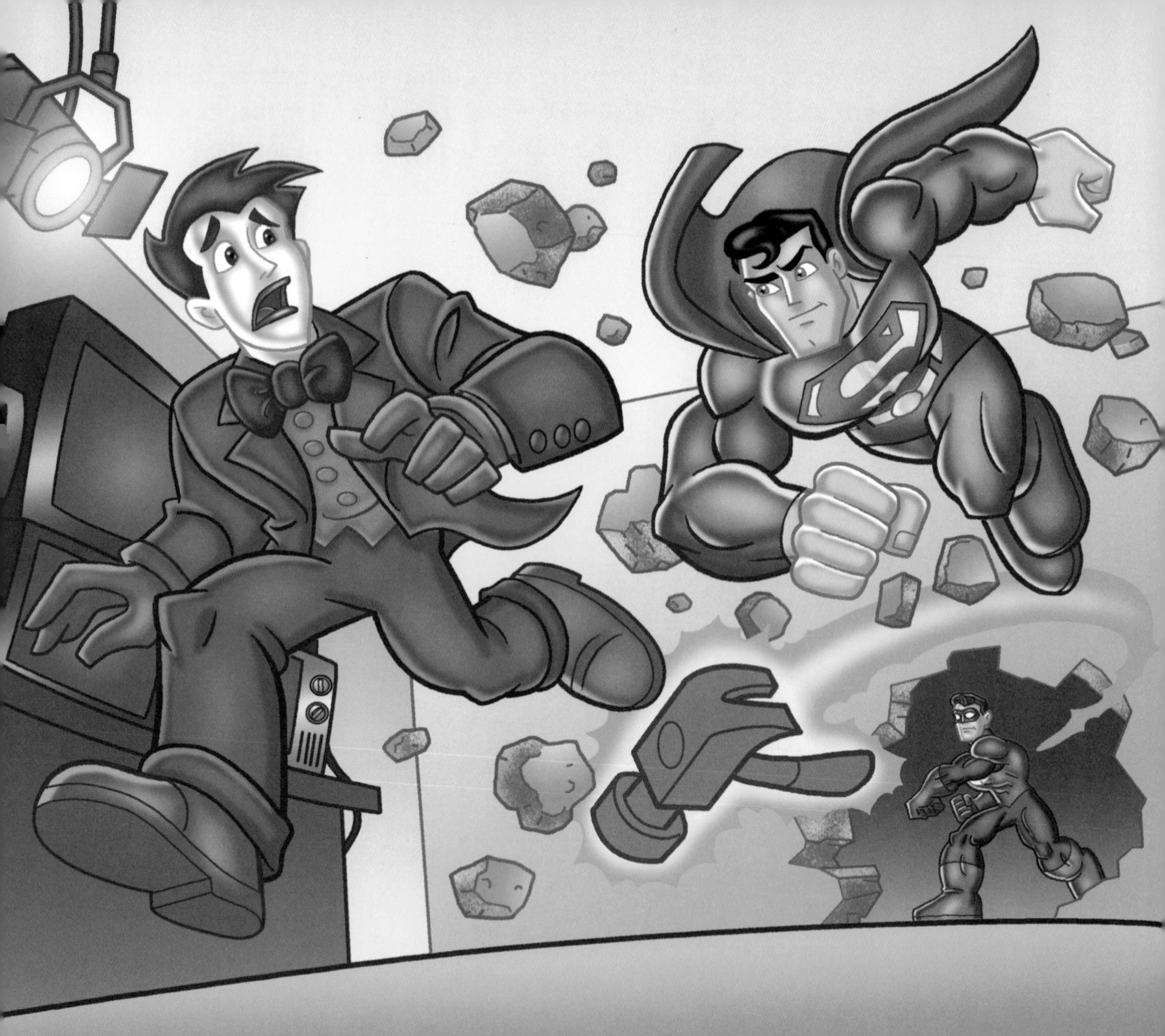

Suddenly, Green Lantern smashed through the wall of the Joker's hideout!
"The show's over," Superman said, flying in behind him.
The Joker ran as fast as he could.

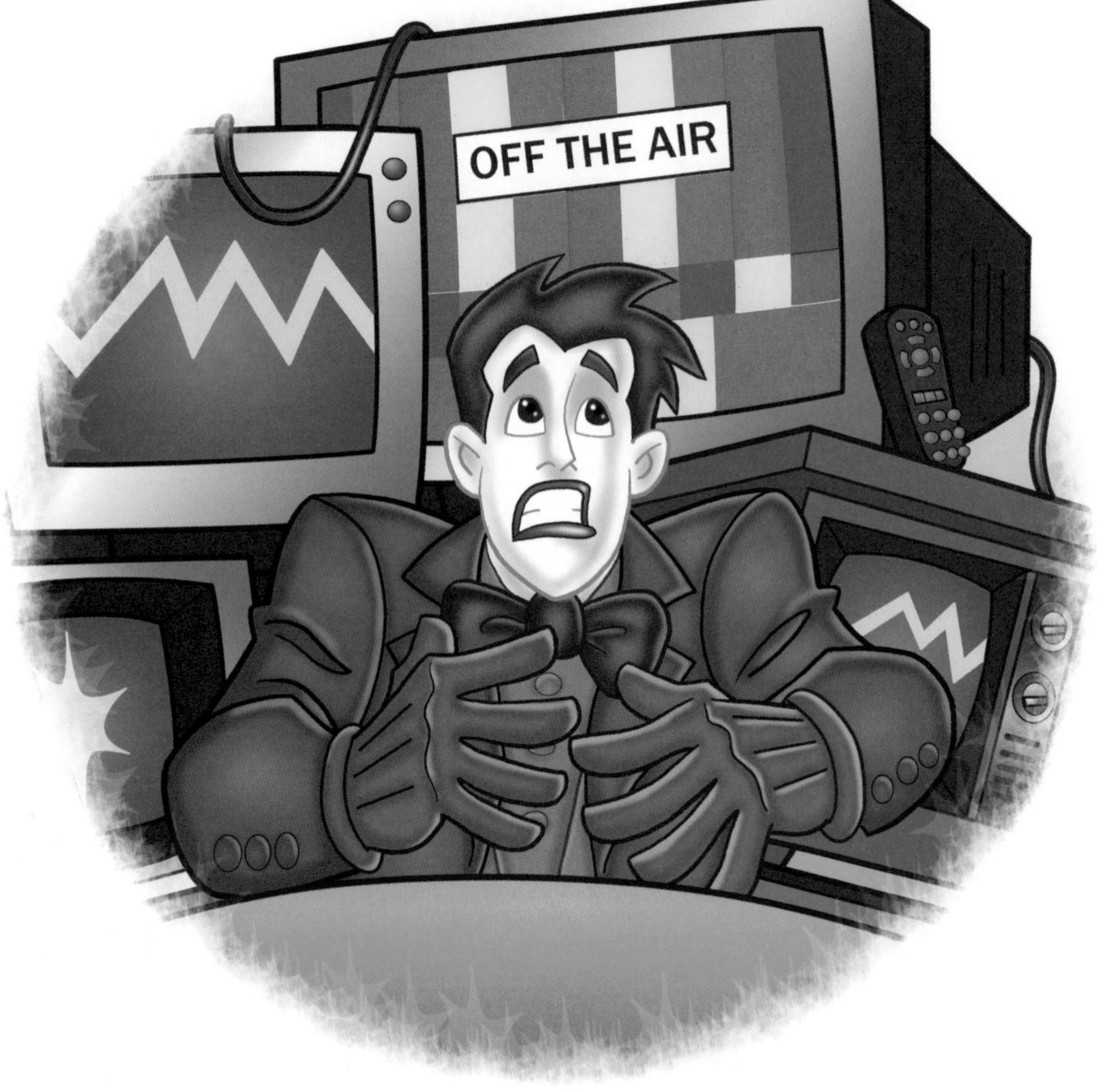
OFF THE AIR

"Joker TV has it all. Action. Drama. Suspense. Me!" the Joker said happily. Then he noticed that one by one, his screens were going blank. "Hey, where's my signal?"

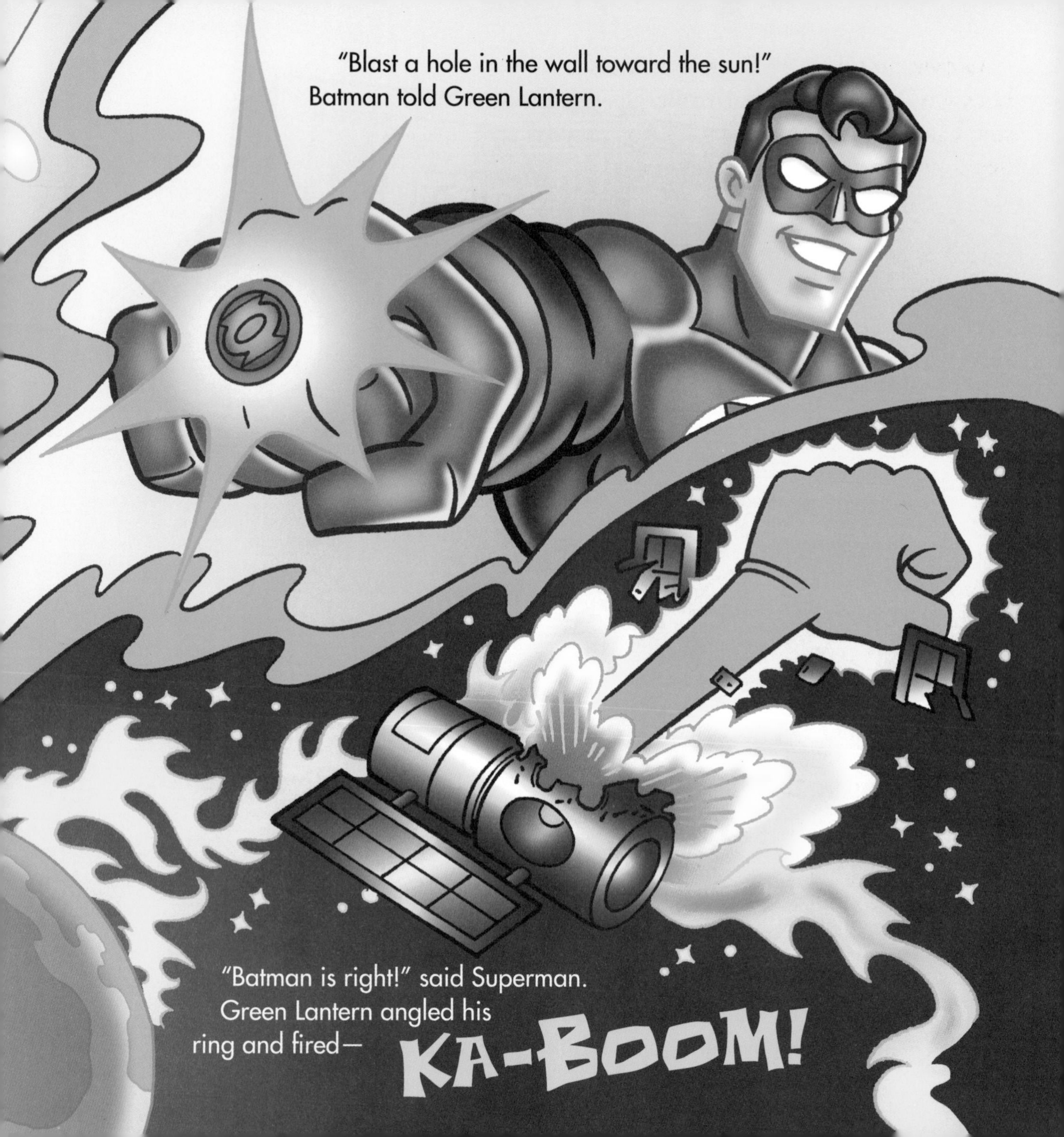

"Blast a hole in the wall toward the sun!" Batman told Green Lantern.

"Batman is right!" said Superman. Green Lantern angled his ring and fired—KA-BOOM!

Gravity smashed the Super Friends against the back wall of the rocket as it roared toward the sun. The Kryptonite in the Joker's doll made even Superman too weak to resist the force.

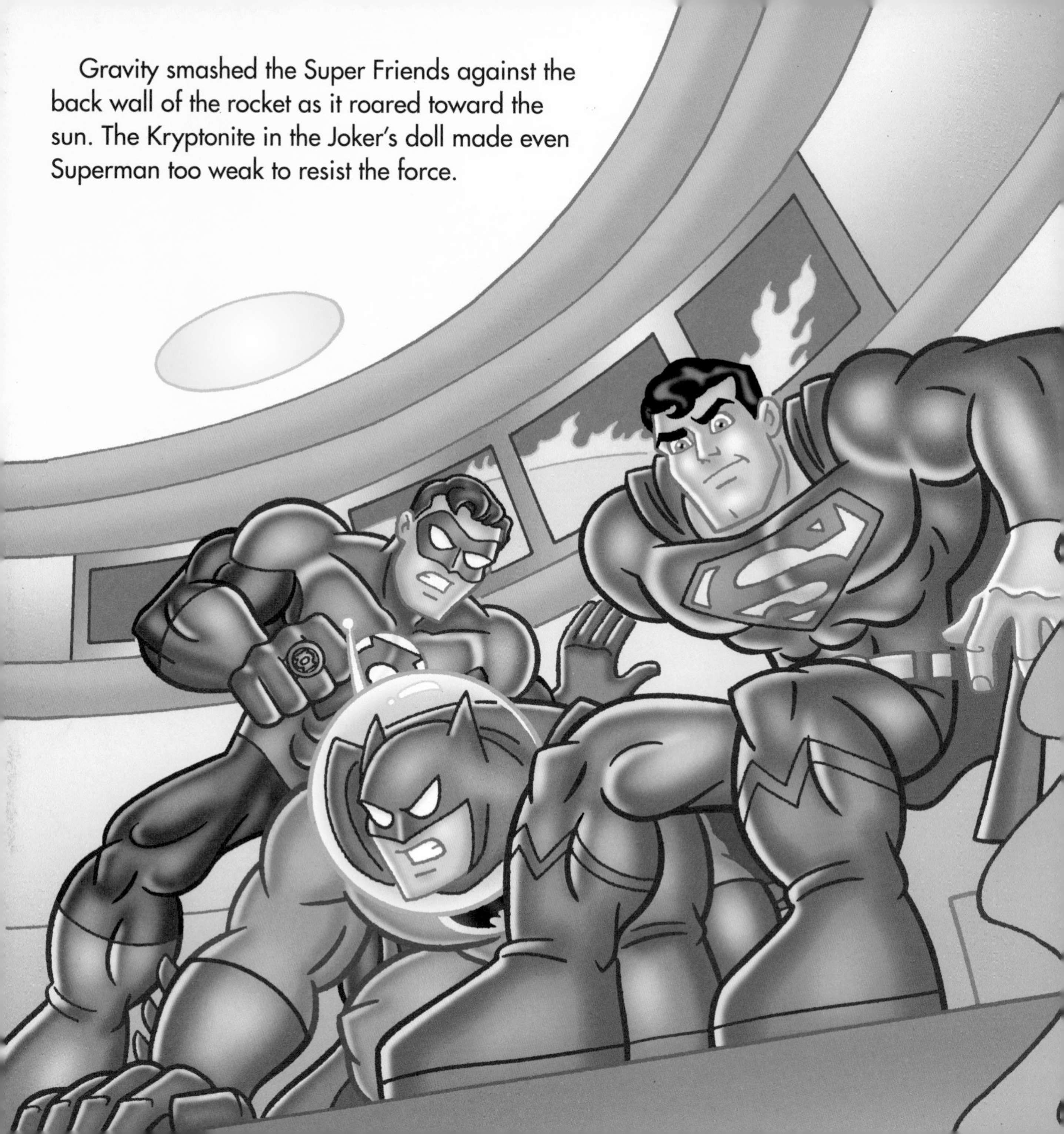

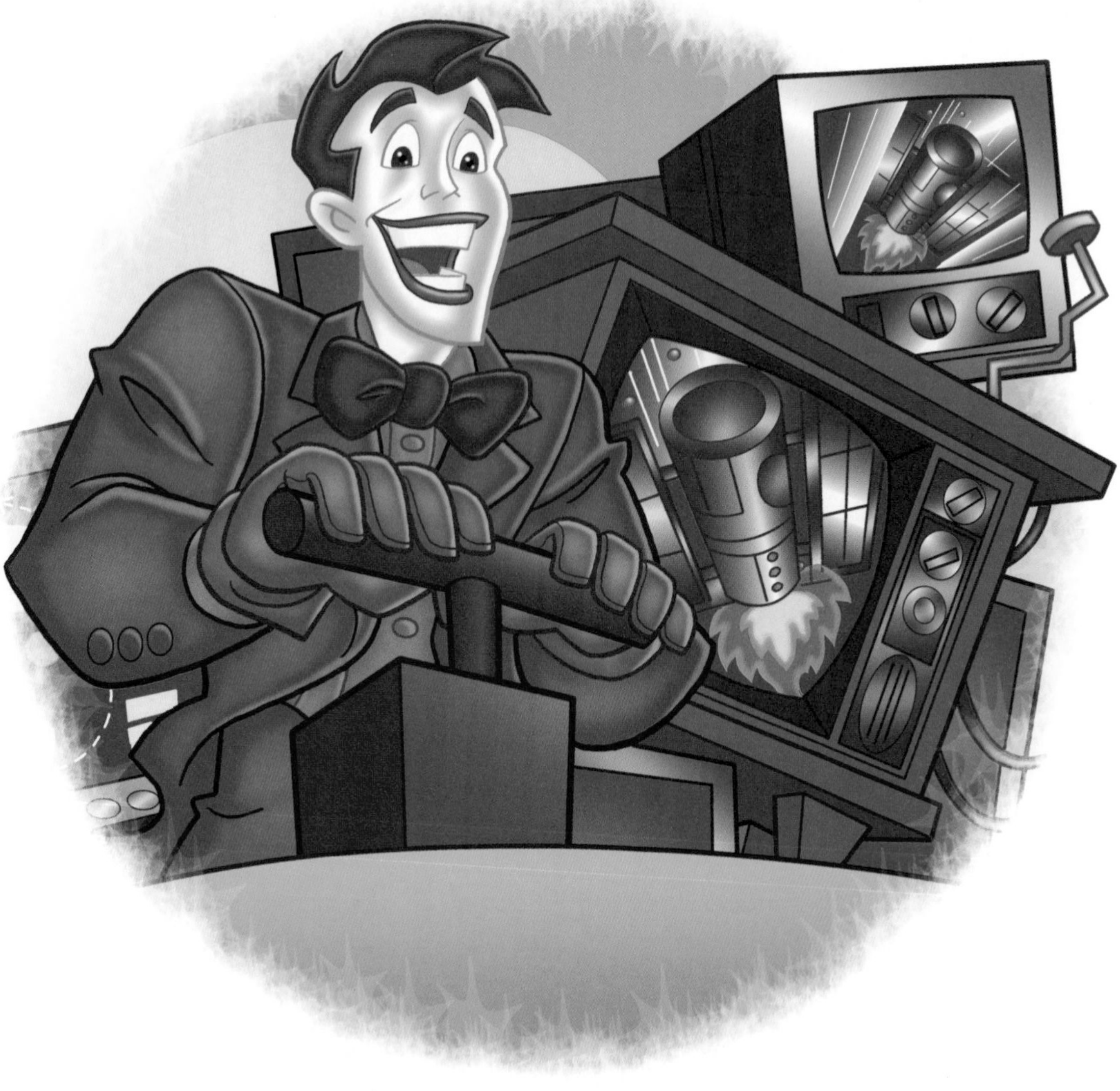

"Three . . . two . . . one!" the Joker said, laughing as he pushed a plunger to ignite the thrusters. "Enjoy being stars!"

Before the Super Friends could react, the rocket blasted off into deep space.

"Surprise!" said the Joker on a video screen. "This isn't a satellite, it's a rocket! And it's about to take you on a one-way trip to the sun! To keep you company, I made you a little me full of Kryptonite—"

"The only substance that can harm Superman!" Batman gasped.

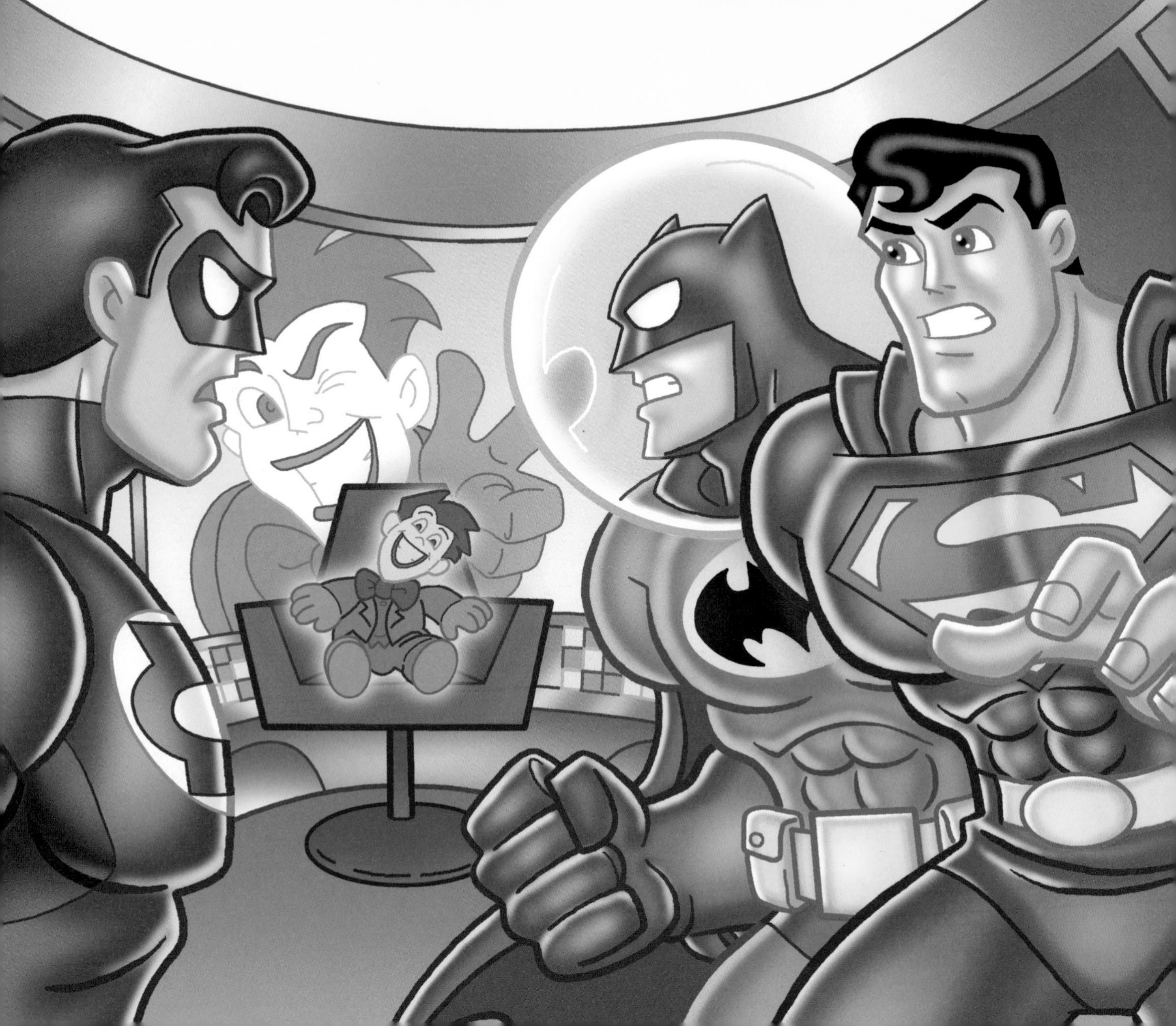

Superman reached the satellite first. With his super-strength, he pulled the air-lock doors apart. "The only close-up *you're* going to see," he said, "is your own prison mug shot when we take you back to jail!"

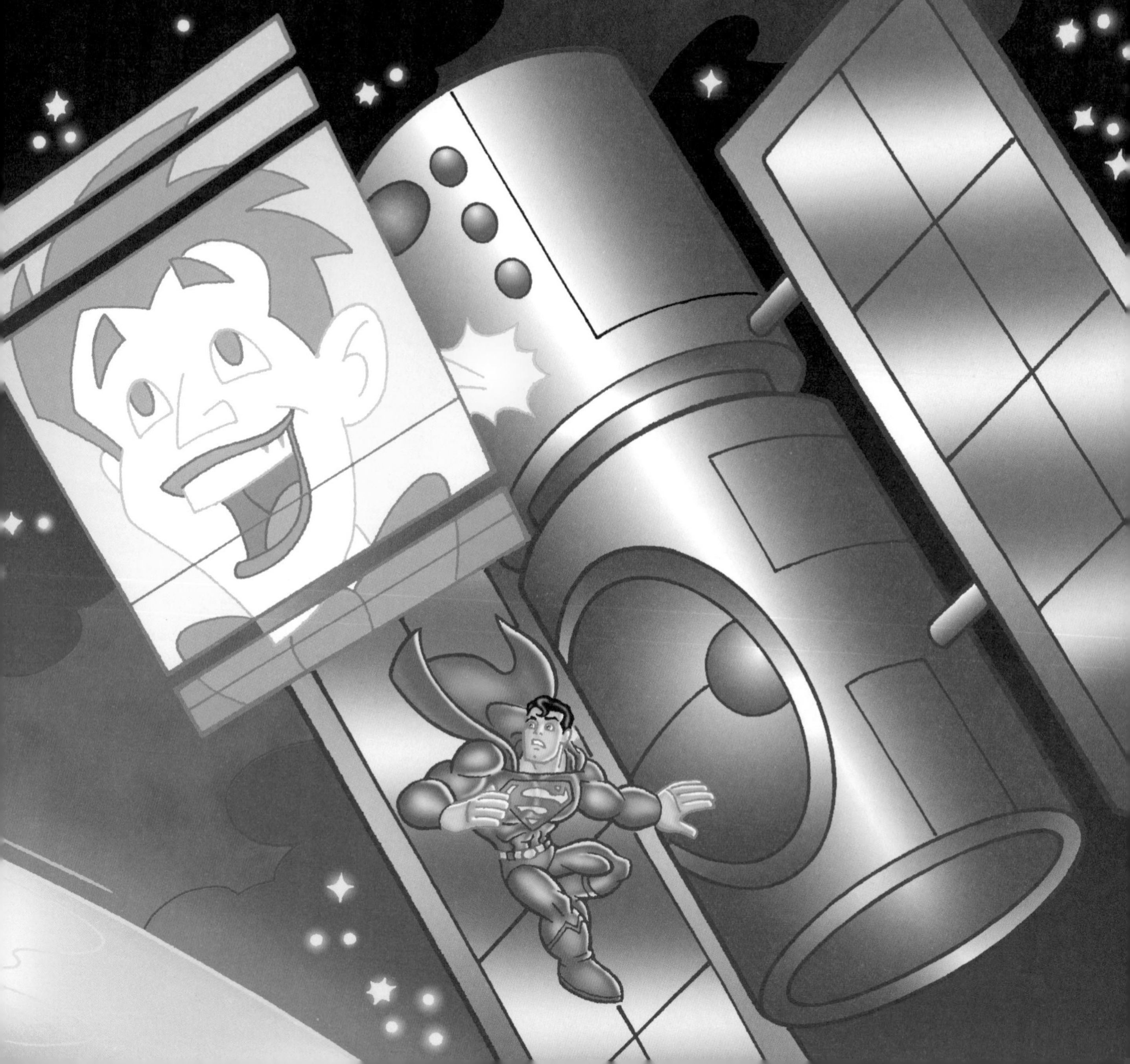

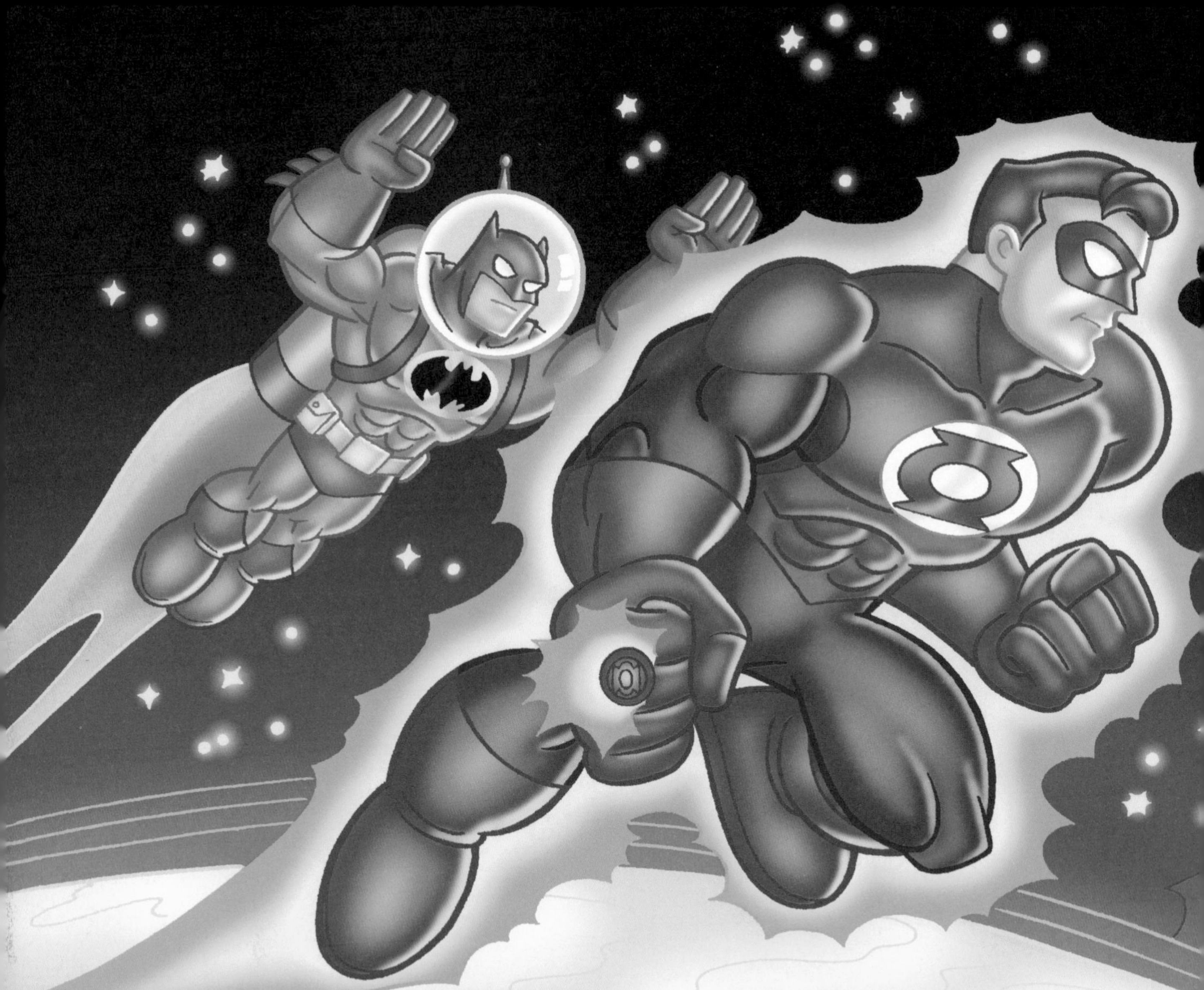

Batman, Superman, and Green Lantern flew into space and quickly located the satellite. A hologram of the Joker's broadcast popped up as they approached.

"Looks like the Super Friends are ready for a close-up," the Joker said to his television audience.

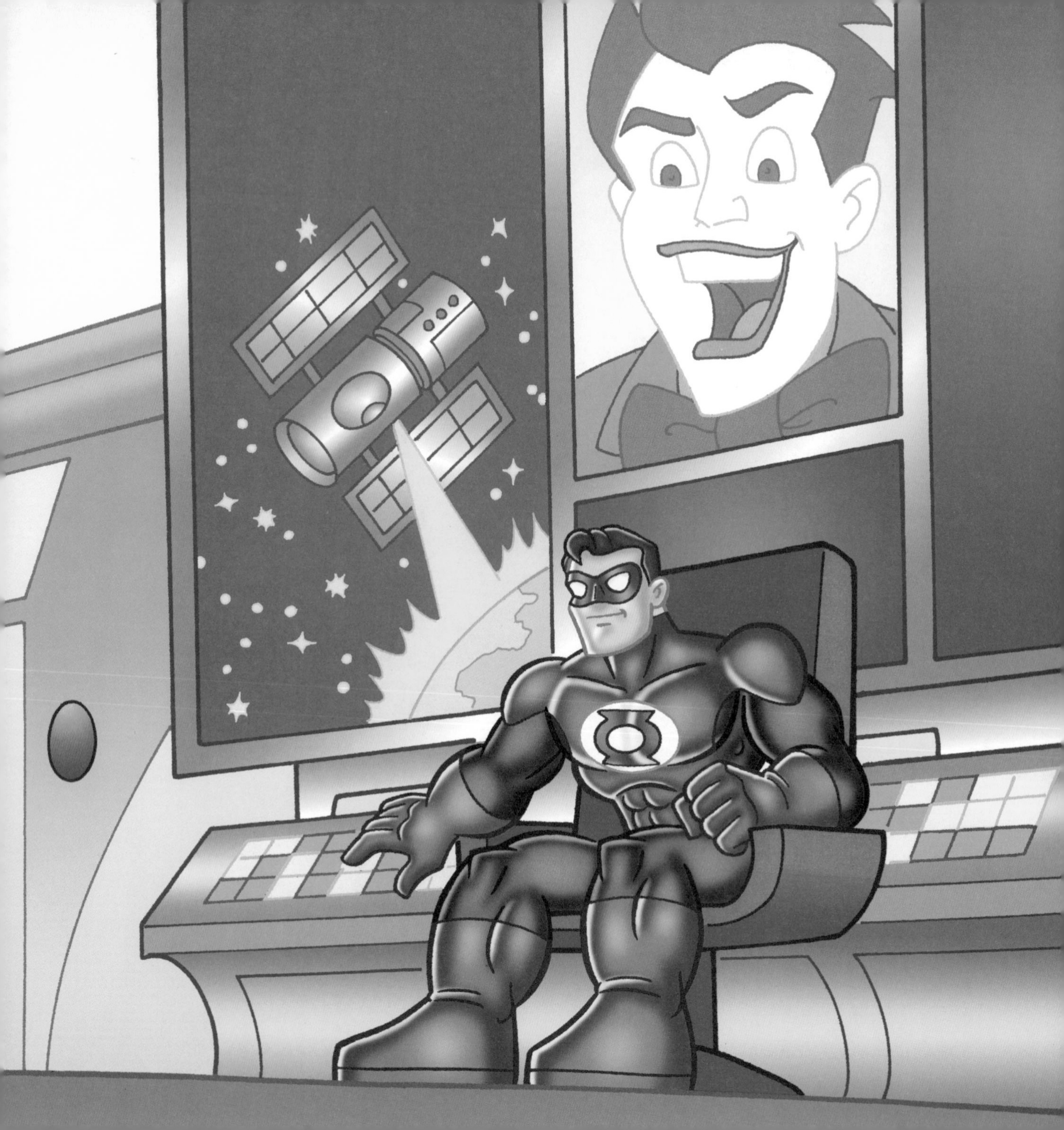

"The first thing we have to do is find that satellite," Batman said to Superman and Green Lantern in their secret headquarters.

"And then we'll turn Joker TV off at the source!" added Green Lantern.

"The Batcomputer has calculated the location of the satellite," said Batman. "I'll get my space helmet and jet pack."

"Let's go!" said Superman.

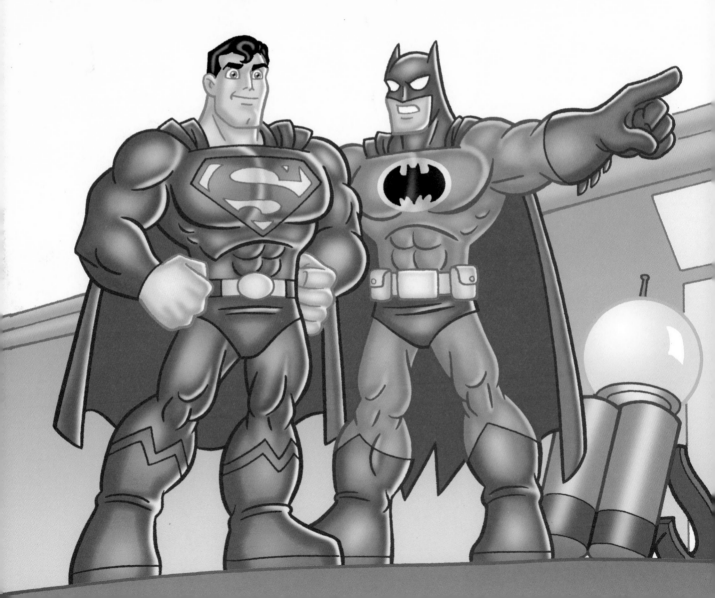

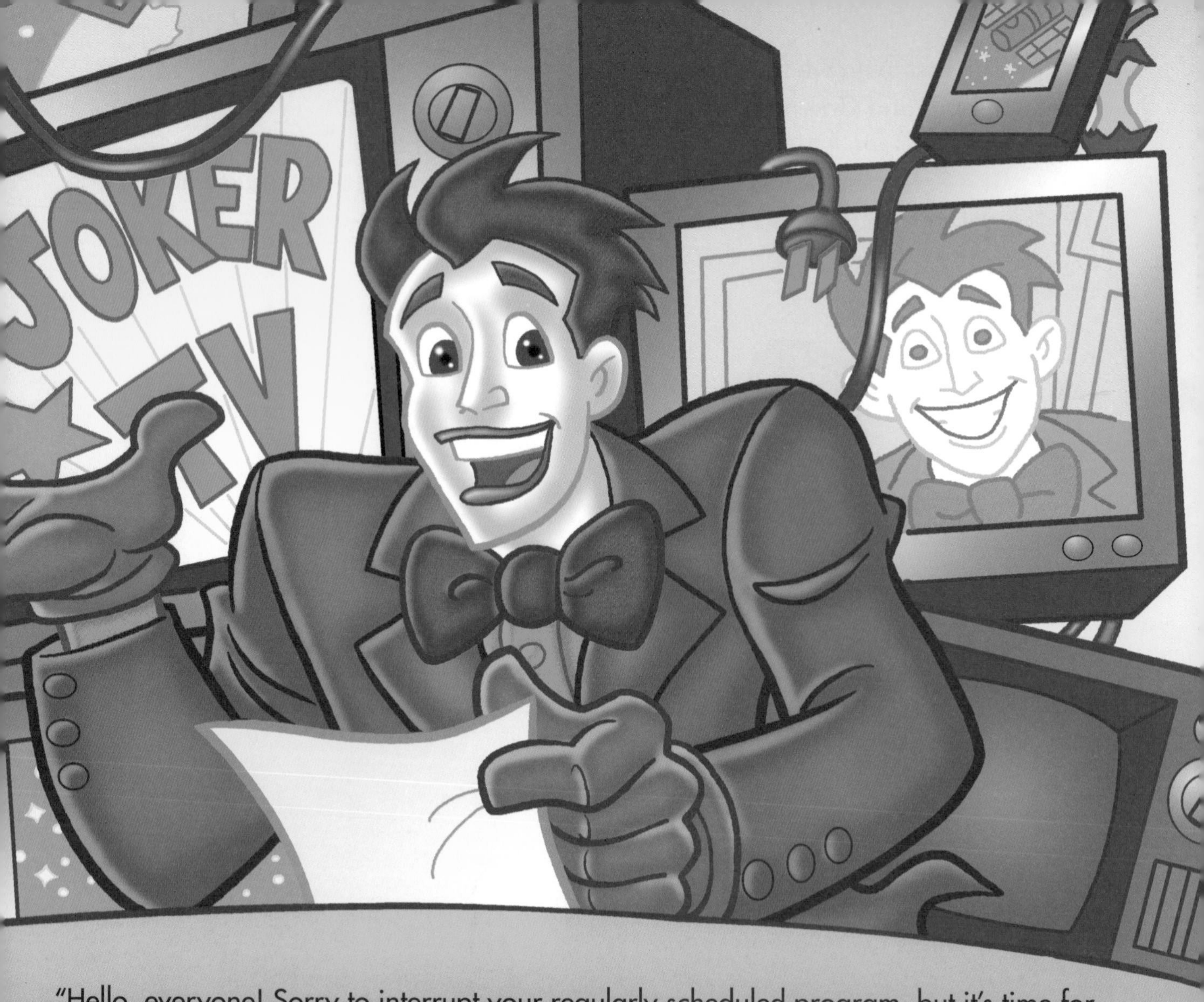
JOKER
TV

"Hello, everyone! Sorry to interrupt your regularly scheduled program, but it's time for Joker TV!" the Joker said to everyone watching television in Gotham. "I'm broadcasting from outer space in my very own satellite, so there'll be no pesky Super Friends to get between you, me, and the TV! HA! HA! HA!"

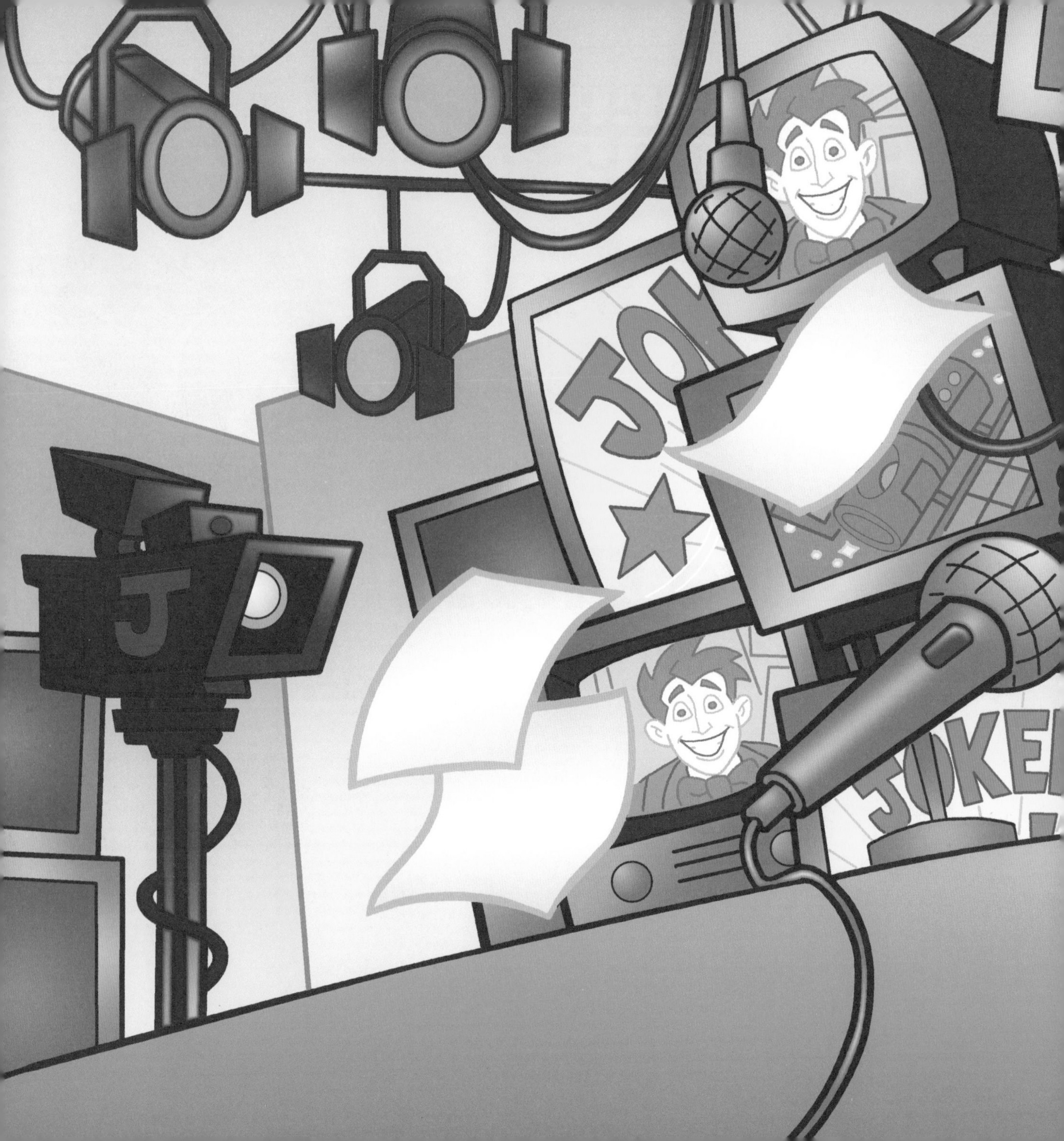

Space Chase!

By Billy Wrecks

Illustrated by Erik Doescher, Mike DeCarlo, and David Tanguay

Random House 🏠 New York

Copyright © 2013 DC Comics.
DC SUPER FRIENDS and all related characters
and elements are trademarks of and © DC Comics.
WB SHIELD: TM & © Warner Bros. Entertainment Inc.
(s13)

RHUS26394

Published in the United States by Random House Children's Books, a division of Random House, Inc.,
1745 Broadway, New York, NY 10019, and in Canada by Random House of Canada Limited, Toronto.
ISBN: 978-0-307-97616-1   randomhouse.com/kids   dckids.kidswb.com   MANUFACTURED IN CHINA
10 9 8 7 6 5 4 3 2